"Are you sure you ... Jamilah?"

She faced him and could see the intense glitter of his eyes, the way a muscle pulsed in his jaw. Slowly, as if she might scare him off, she nodded her head. "Yes, I want to know, Salman."

Salman looked into Jamilah's eyes. He had a bizarre sensation of drowning, while at the same time clinging onto a life raft. Was he really about to divulge to her what no one else knew? His deepest, darkest shame? Yet in that instant he knew an overwhelming need to unburden himself to her. It could never be with anyone else. He saw that now, as clear as day.

All about the author…
Abby Green

ABBY GREEN deferred doing a social anthropology degree to work freelance as an assistant director in the film and TV industry—which is a social study in itself! Since then it's been early starts, long hours, mucky fields, ugly car parks and wet-weather gear—especially working in Ireland.

She has no bona fide qualifications, but could probably help negotiate a peace agreement between two warring countries after years of dealing with recalcitrant actors. She discovered a guide to writing romance one day, and decided to capitalize on her longtime love for Harlequin romances and attempt to follow in the footsteps of such authors as Kate Walker and Penny Jordan. She's enjoying the excuse to be paid to sit inside, away from the elements. She lives in Dublin and hopes that you will enjoy her stories.

You can email her at abbygreen3@yahoo.co.uk.

Other titles by Abby Green available in ebook:

Harlequin Presents

3012—THE STOLEN BRIDE*
2979—IN CHRISTOPHIDES' KEEPING

*The Notorious Wolfes

Abby Green

SECRETS OF THE OASIS

TORONTO NEW YORK LONDON
AMSTERDAM PARIS SYDNEY HAMBURG
STOCKHOLM ATHENS TOKYO MILAN MADRID
PRAGUE WARSAW BUDAPEST AUCKLAND

Recycling programs
for this product may
not exist in your area.

ISBN-13: 978-0-373-13046-7

SECRETS OF THE OASIS

First North American Publication 2012

Copyright © 2011 by Abby Green

SECRETS OF THE OASIS

PROLOGUE

A SIX-YEAR-OLD girl stands at a graveside, on her own. Her face is deathly pale, her blue eyes huge and shimmering with unshed tears, her hair a sleek waterfall of black down to her waist. A dark, handsome boy, Salman, detaches himself from the larger group and comes over to take her hand.

He looks at her solemnly, too solemn for his twelve years. 'Don't cry, Jamilah, you have to be strong now.'

She just looks at him. His parents died in the same plane crash as hers. If he can be strong, so can she. She blinks back the tears and nods briefly, once, and doesn't take her eyes off him even when he looks away to where his own parents have just been buried. Their hands stay tightly clasped together.

CHAPTER ONE

Six years ago, Paris.

JAMILAH MOREAU had to restrain herself from turning her walk into a light-hearted skip as she walked up the French boulevard with the Eiffel Tower in the distance. She grimaced at herself. It was such a cliché but it was Paris, it was springtime, and she was in love. She wanted to throw her bags of shopping in the air and laugh out loud, and turn her face up to the blossoms floating lazily to the ground from the trees.

She wanted to hug everyone. She forced back an irrepressible grin. She'd always thought people over-exaggerated Paris's romantic allure, but now she knew why. You had to be in love to get it. No wonder her French father and Merkazadi mother had fallen in love here—how could they not have?

She was unaware of the admiring looks her jet-black hair, exotic olive-skinned colouring and startlingly blue eyes drew from people passing by—both men and women. Her heart was beating so fast with excitement that she knew she had to calm herself. But all she felt like doing was shouting out to the world with arms wide: *I'm in love with Salman al Saqr and he loves me, too!*

At that thought, though, her step faltered slightly and

her conscience pricked. He hadn't actually *said* he loved her. Not even when she'd told him she loved him that morning, as they'd lain in bed, when Jamilah had felt as if she'd expire with happiness and sensual satedness. She couldn't have held it back any longer. The words had been trembling on her lips for days.

Three weeks. That was all it had been since she'd literally bumped into Salman in the street, when she'd emerged from the university where she'd just finished her final exams. She'd practically grown up with him, but hadn't seen him in a few years, and a seismic reaction had washed through her at seeing the object of her lifelong crush. As darkly handsome as he'd ever been, and even more so. Because now he was a man. Tall, broad, and powerful.

His hands had wrapped around her arms to steady her, and he'd been about to let her go, with a thrillingly appreciative gleam in his dark gaze, when suddenly those black brows had drawn together, his eyes had narrowed and he'd snapped out disbelievingly, *'Jamilah?'* She'd nodded, her heart thumping and a hot blush rising up through her body. She'd fantasised about him looking at her like that for so long…

They'd gone for a coffee. When they'd stood in the street afterwards she'd been about to walk away, feeling as though her heart was being torn from her chest, when Salman had stopped her and said quickly, 'Wait…have dinner with me tonight?'

And that had been the start of the most magical three weeks of her life. She'd said yes quickly. Too quickly. Jamilah grimaced again as a dose of reality hit. She should have been more cool, more sophisticated…but it would have been impossible after years of idolising him from afar—a childhood crush which had developed into teenage obsession and now adult longing.

That first weekend Salman had taken her back to his apartment and made love to her for the first time… and even now a deep flowing heat invaded her lower body, making her blush as X-rated images flooded her mind.

She shook her head to dispel the images, kept walking. She was on her way to his apartment now, to cook him dinner. Her conscience struck again. Salman hadn't actually invited her over this evening—in fact he'd been unusually quiet that morning. But Jamilah was confident that when he saw her, saw the delicious supplies she'd bought, he'd smile that sexy, crooked smile and open his door wide.

As she waited to cross the busy road across from his imposing eighteenth-century apartment building she thought of the instances when she'd seen an intense darkness pervade Salman—whenever she mentioned Merkazad, where they were both from, or his older brother Sheikh Nadim, ruler of Merkazad.

Salman had always had an innate darkness, but it had never intimidated Jamilah. From as far back as she could remember she'd felt an affinity with him, and had never questioned the fact that he was a loner and didn't seem to share the social ease of his older brother. But in the past few weeks Jamilah had quickly learnt to avoid talking of Nadim or Merkazad.

She was due to return to Merkazad in a week's time, but she was going to tell Salman tonight that if he wanted her to stay in Paris she would. It wasn't what she'd planned at all, but the anatomy of her world had changed utterly since she'd met him again.

She arrived at the ornate door of Salman's building,

where he lived on the top floor in a stunning open-plan apartment. The concierge started to greet her warmly when she came in, but then a look flashed over his face and he said, '*Excusez-moi, mademoiselle,* but is the Sheikh expecting you this evening?'

Hearing Salman being described as 'the Sheikh' gave Jamilah a little jolt; she'd almost forgotten about his status as next in line to be ruler of Merkazad after Nadim. Merkazad was a small independent sheikhdom within the bigger country of Al-Omar on the Arabian peninsula. It had been her mother's home and birthplace, where Jamilah had been brought up after her birth in Paris. Her French father had worked for Salman's father as an advisor.

Jamilah smiled widely and held up the bulging bags of shopping. 'I'm cooking dinner.'

The concierge smiled back, but he looked a little uncomfortable, and a shiver of unease went down Jamilah's spine for no good reason as the lift ascended. When it came to a smooth halt and the doors opened the trickle of unease got stronger. Salman's door was partially open, and she heard a deep-throated, very feminine chuckle just as she pushed it open fully.

It took a few seconds for the scene in front of her to register. Salman was standing with his head bent, about to kiss a very beautiful red-haired woman who was twined around him like a climbing vine. Jamilah suddenly felt stupidly self-conscious in her student uniform of jeans and T-shirt.

Their mouths met, and Salman's hands were on the woman's slender waist as he hauled her closer. Exactly the way he had done with Jamilah. She must have made a sound or something—it was only afterwards that she'd realised that was the moment she'd dropped the shopping.

Salman broke off the kiss and looked round. But, Jamilah noted, he didn't take his hands off the woman, who was now looking at her, too, her beautiful green eyes flashing at the interruption.

Jamilah barely registered Salman's thick dark unruly hair, which had always curled a touch too near his collar, or his intensely dark flashing eyes, which she'd always thought held a universe of shadows and secrets. The hard line of his jaw, and his exquisitely sculpted cheekbones which somehow didn't diminish the harsh masculinity of his face, were all peripheral to her shock.

Numb with that shock, and a million and one other things all at once, Jamilah just stood stupidly and watched Salman say something low and succinct to the woman, who gave a little moue of displeasure before she stepped back and picked up her bag and coat.

She brushed past Jamilah on her way out, trailing a noxious cloud of perfume behind her, and said huskily, *'Je te voir plus tard, cheri.'*

See you later, darling.

The door closed behind Jamilah and reaction started to set in. Salman faced her now, hands on narrow hips, dressed in a dark suit, crisp shirt and tie. It was the first time she'd seen him dressed so formally, and it made him look austere. She knew that he was an investment banker, but he'd never really discussed it. She realised now he'd never really discussed anything personal with her—just seduced her to within an inch of her life.

Jamilah could feel a trembling starting up in her legs, but before she could speak Salman said curtly, 'I didn't expect to see you this evening. We made no arrangement.'

They'd made no arrangement to turn her life upside down in the space of three weeks, either! Jamilah's numb brain was trying to equate this distant stranger with the man who had made love to her less than twelve hours before. The same man who had whispered words of endearment in her ears as he'd thrust so deeply inside her that she'd arched her back and gasped out loud, raking her nails down his back to his buttocks.

She fought to block the images and felt like crying. 'I... wanted to surprise you. I was going to cook dinner...'

Jamilah looked down then, to see carnage. Broken eggs seeped all over the parquet floor. A bottle of wine, which thankfully hadn't broken, lolled on its side. She looked up again jerkily when Salman said, 'You can't just wander in here when you feel like it, Jamilah.'

A muscle ticking in his jaw showed his displeasure. And, from a depth she'd not known she had, a self-preserving instinct kicked in. Jamilah hitched up her chin minutely, even as her world started to crumble around her.

'Of course I wouldn't have come if I'd known that you would be...*busy.*' And then she couldn't help asking. 'Were you...?' A poison-tipped arrow pierced her heart. 'Were you seeing *her* while you were seeing me?'

Salman shook his head briefly, abruptly. Impatiently. 'No.'

Jamilah said through numb lips, 'Clearly, though, you're seeing her *now.* Evidently you've already grown bored. Three weeks must be your limit.'

She was aware of the raw pain throbbing through her voice. She couldn't hold it back. Not for the life of her. All she could think of was how she'd bared her heart and soul to this man in the early dawn hours. She'd said hesitantly, huskily, *'I love you, Salman. I think I've always loved you.'*

He'd smiled his lopsided smile and said, 'Don't be ridiculous. You barely know me.'

Jamilah had been fierce. 'I've known you all my life, Salman…and I know that I love you.' And that was when he'd pulled back and become monosyllabic. She could see it now, clear as day.

Salman asked now, with fatal softness, 'Just what exactly were you expecting, Jamilah?'

Jamilah shut her emotions away. 'Nothing. It would have been stupid of me to expect anything, wouldn't it? You're already moving on. Were you even going to tell me?'

Salman's mouth thinned. 'What's to tell? We've had an enjoyable fling. In one week you're going back to Merkazad, and, yes, of course I'll be moving on.'

Jamilah felt herself recoil inwardly, as if from a blow. This man had been her first lover…to call what had happened between them a *fling* reduced every moment to a travesty. Reduced the gift of her innocence that she'd given him to nothing.

Salman frowned and took a step closer. 'You *are* going back to Merkazad, aren't you?' He cursed under his breath—an Arabic curse that Jamilah had only heard in the souks of Merkazad amongst men—and said harshly, 'You didn't seriously expect anything more, did you?'

Her face must have been giving her away spectacularly, despite her best efforts, because then he said, with chilling devastation, 'I never promised you anything. I never gave you any hint to expect anything more, did I?'

She shook her head on auto-pilot. No, he hadn't. The

utter devastation of his words sank in somewhere deep and vulnerable. It took all of Jamilah's strength just to stay standing. He couldn't know how much he was hurting her. She'd played with fire and she was getting burnt by a master. Every day had been heady, magical, but at no point had Salman made a plan anything more than twenty-four hours in advance. Now she just wanted to leave and curl up into a ball, far away, where she could curse her own naivety. But she couldn't move.

Salman watched the woman before him. He'd cut himself off from any kind of emotion so long ago that he almost didn't recognise it now, as it struggled to break through. An aching pain constricted his chest, but he ruthlessly pushed it down. For the past three weeks he'd indulged in a haze of unreality, in believing that perhaps he wasn't as damned as he'd always believed. Bumping into Jamilah, seeing her again—seeing how utterly beautiful she'd become—had broken something open inside him. He'd had the gall to think for a second that some of her innately pure goodness could rub off on him.

When he'd seen Jamilah cross the street minutes before, a huge grin on her face, he'd realised that she'd meant what she'd said that morning—she *was* in love with him. He'd tried to block her words out all day, tried to reassure himself that she hadn't meant it… tried to ignore the uncomfortable feeling of guilt and responsibility.

He'd felt in that moment as he'd watched her approach his apartment as if he was holding a tiny, delicate butterfly in his hands, which he could not fail to crush—even if he wanted to protect its fragile beauty.

Eloise, his colleague, who had followed him up to his apartment on the flimsy pretext of getting a document, had come on to him at that exact moment, her brash, over-confident sexuality in direct contrast to the subtle sensuality of the woman approaching his apartment. In that moment he'd known he had to let Jamilah go… so comprehensively that she would be left in no doubt that it was over. So when his concierge had confirmed that Jamilah was indeed coming up, he'd felt something shut down inside him. He would crush the butterfly to pieces. Because he had no choice—had nothing to offer other than a battered soul riven with dark secrets. He could not love.

For a long moment Salman said nothing, just looked at Jamilah until she felt dizzy. Perhaps she'd imagined the awful scene? His frosty manner? *That woman…* For a second she thought she saw something like regret in his eyes, but then Salman finally spoke, and he stuck the knife in so deep that Jamilah felt her heart slice in two.

'I knew you were coming up. The concierge warned me.' He shrugged, and she knew in that moment what real cruelty looked like. 'I could have stopped myself from kissing Eloise, but I figured what was the point? Better that you find out now the kind of person I am.'

He twisted the knife.

'This never should have happened. It was weak of me to seduce you.'

Immediately Jamilah read between those words: what he meant was it had been all too *easy* to seduce her.

'You should leave. I imagine you have plenty to pre-pare for going back to Merkazad.' His mouth was a thin line now. 'Believe me, Jamilah, I'm not the kind of man who can give you what you want. I'm dark and twisted inside—not a knight in shining armour who will whisk you away into a romantic dream. This is over. I'll be taking Eloise out tonight and getting on with my life. I suggest that you do the same.'

Numb all over, Jamilah said threadily, 'I thought we were friends… I thought…'

'What?' he said harshly. 'That just because we grew up in the same place and spent time together we would be friends for life?'

Something inside Jamilah wasn't obeying her mental command to just shut up. 'It was more than that… What we had was different. You spoke to me, spent time with me when you wouldn't with anyone else… This last three weeks…I thought what we'd always shared had grown into something…'

A look of forbidding cold bleakness crossed Salman's face, and finally Jamilah curbed her tongue, wondering why on earth she was laying herself bare like this.

'You followed me around like a besotted puppy dog for years and I never had the heart to tell you to leave me alone. This last three weeks was about lust, pure and simple. You've grown into a beautiful woman and I desired you. Nothing more, nothing less.'

That was it. Whatever feelings Jamilah might have harboured for Salman over the years froze and withered to dust inside her. He'd also destroyed any halcyon memories she'd had of a bond between them. She forced words out through the excruciating pain. 'You don't need to say any more. I get the message. Whatever heart you may have once had is clearly gone. You're nothing but a cold bastard.'

'Yes, I am,' Salman agreed, with an indefinable edge to his voice.

Jamilah finally managed to move, and turned round to go, stepping out of the destruction of the fallen shopping around her. She couldn't even attempt to pick it up.

At the door she heard Salman say, with cynicism ringing in his voice, 'Say hello to my beloved brother and Merkazad for me. I don't intend seeing either any time soon.'

Or you. He didn't have to say the words. They hung in the air. Jamilah opened the door and walked out, and didn't look back once.

One year ago.

The Sultan of Al-Omar's birthday celebrations were as lavish as ever. They were taking place in the stunning Hussein Palace, which was in the heart of the glittering metropolis of B'harani, right on the coast of the Arabian peninsula, about two hours drive from mountainous Merkazad.

One of the Sultan's aides had been pursuing Jamilah on and off for years, and she'd finally relented and agreed to come to the party as his date. Her belly clenched now, because she had to acknowledge that the main motivation behind her decision to come was because Salman was going to be there.

Each year the tabloids across the globe exulted in reporting feverishly on which A-list beauty he'd decided to take as his new mistress. He never came to the party with anyone, but he always left with someone.

Her date had left her side for a moment in the thronged ballroom. It was the first night of celebrations which were meant to be for family and close friends only, but approximately two hundred people milled about the room.

Jamilah's skin prickled, and she cursed herself for

her rash decision. She'd taken it because in all the years since she'd last seen Salman in Paris she hadn't been able to get him out of her head, and she'd started having dreams again. Dreams of when she was six years old and standing at her parents' grave, when Salman had come to take her hand and infused her with a strength so palpable she'd never forgotten it.

She knew it was ridiculous, but she'd fallen in love with him at that moment. And even though she'd long since disabused herself of the notion that that childish love had grown and developed into something deeper, she couldn't help her heart clenching at the evocative memory.

She cringed inwardly now when she thought of how her teenage years had been lifted out of the doldrums every time Salman had made a visit home from school in the UK, and she, tongue-tied and blushing, had been reduced to a puddle of hormones. But then his visits had become more and more infrequent, until he'd stopping coming home at all, turning her world lacklustre and dull.

She didn't have to be reminded of how Salman had regarded her lovesick attentions. It was bad enough that her motivation for going to Paris to study had had as much to do with the fact that Salman lived there than because it had always been her father's wish that she study in his home city. And she'd paid heavily for that decision.

Bitterness flooded her.

The dreams were the last straw. She couldn't go on like this, so she'd hoped that if she came to the party, if she saw Salman living the debauched lifestyle of the notorious playboy Sheikh that he was, he'd disgust her and she'd be able to move on. At least enough to feel some measure of closure.

She'd imagined greeting Salman with a look of practised surprise, a tiny smile of recognition. Not a hint of the emotional turmoil she'd suffered these past years would show on her face or in her eyes. She'd ask him how he was, while affecting a look of mild boredom, and then, with a perfunctory platitude, she'd drift away and that would be it. She would be over him. And he would be left in no doubt that their brief affair meant nothing to her at all...

Except it hadn't happened like that. As she'd been leaving her room she'd looked up from her bag, distracted, to see a tall, dark, broad figure in a tuxedo ahead of her. She'd nearly called out, because she'd thought it was his brother, Nadim. They shared the same height and build. But then she'd realised her mistake and it had been too late as a sound emerged from her mouth.

She'd had a first fleeting impression of him, cutting a lonely, solitary figure, and then he'd turned round with a frown on his face which had only grown more marked as he'd registered who she was. Jamilah had been too shocked and stunned at being faced with him like that in an empty corridor to say anything.

He'd rocked back on his heels, hands in the pockets of his trousers, and whatever fleeting hint of vulnerability she might have sensed about him had been smashed to pieces as his gaze had dropped down her body with lazy, sensual appraisal. 'Jamilah...we finally meet again. I was wondering if you'd been avoiding me.'

His deep, drawling voice had impacted upon her somewhere deep and visceral, and for one awful moment Jamilah had been transported back in time to that devastating evening in Paris, in his apartment. She'd given up any hope of sticking to the script she'd perfected in her head. With an iron will, she'd struggled to regain composure and sent up silent thanks for the armour of a designer dress and make-up. She'd forced herself to move, stride forward, fully intending to walk past him, but he'd caught her arm and the feel of his hand on her bare skin had caused her to stumble.

She'd looked up at him, and her treacherous heart had beat fast—too fast. 'Don't be ridiculous, Salman. Why on earth would I be avoiding you?'

An inner voice answered: *Because he broke your heart into tiny pieces and you've never forgotten it.*

Jamilah noticed then that faint grooves were worn into the brackets of his mouth. His eyes were hard—far harder than she remembered them being.

'Because I've never seen you at the Sultan's party before.'

Jamilah wrenched her arm free. 'This isn't exactly my scene. And, not that it's any of your business, I decided to come tonight because I was invited by—'

'Ah, Jamilah, there you are. I was just coming to collect you.'

With a rolling wave of relief, Jamilah saw her date approach. She let him come and put a proprietorial arm around her shoulder, for once not minding the way men seemed to find it impossible not to stake their claim. And with a few words of muttered incoherency to Salman she let herself be led away, leaving Salman behind.

Now she stood amongst the throng that had gathered after the sumptuous dinner—a dinner Jamilah had had to force down her throat—horribly aware of Salman's intense and assessing gaze from across the table.

To her utter relief, at that moment she spotted Sheikh Nadim and his date, an Irish girl called Iseult, who had come to work in Nadim's stables after he'd bought out her family's stud farm in Ireland.

Jamilah went to join them, and she could see their concerned looks as they took in her pale features. She felt light-headed. And then Iseult confirmed it by asking, 'Jamilah, what is it?'

Jamilah smiled tightly. 'Nothing at all.'

But Jamilah could feel whatever blood was left in her face drain southward when she saw Salman approach with narrowed eyes. No escape. *How* had she ever thought this would be a good idea?

Muttering something about finding her date, Jamilah fled across the room and out to the patio through open doors, where thankfully few people milled about. She rested her hands on the stone balustrade and sucked in deep breaths, only to feel every cell in her body react when she sensed his presence behind her.

She turned slowly and saw that the patio was now empty, as if the sheer force of the tension between her and Salman had repelled everyone else.

Not caring how she might be giving herself away, Jamilah said unevenly, 'Leave me alone, Salman.'

His voice was harsh against the silence. 'If you'd wanted to be left alone you should have stayed in Merkazad.'

Jamilah's mouth twisted to acknowledge that uncomfortable truth. To think she'd ever thought that she could cope with this... 'Ah, yes, because you never come home.'

His eyes flashed but he didn't deny it. 'Exactly.'

For a long moment neither one said anything, and then Salman took a step forward. Jamilah's heart lurched, and she noticed that the patio doors had been closed.

He said, with a rough quality to his voice that

resonated deep inside her, 'You're even more beautiful than I remember.'

Jamilah forgot about escape and glared at Salman. His compliment fell on deaf ears. There was an unmistakably predatory gleam in his eyes and Jamilah railed against it. He had no right. His face was cast into shadow, so she couldn't make out his expression. 'The last time you saw me you told me I was beautiful, Salman—or don't you remember telling me why you took me to bed?'

'You were undeniably beautiful then, but now there's a maturity to your beauty…an edge.' There was something achingly wistful in his voice for a moment, which caught Jamilah off guard.

She forced a mocking smile to numb lips. 'You should be able to recognise cynicism when you see it, Salman. After all you're the King of the Cynics, aren't you? Always coming to the Sultan's party empty-handed and walking away with the most beautiful woman here. Do you still stick to your three-week rule, or was that privilege afforded just to me? Tell me, how long did the lovely Eloise last?'

'Stop it.'

'Why should I?'

Salman stepped closer then, out of the shadows, and when Jamilah saw the starkness of his beautiful features she nearly forgot everything. He blocked out the light behind him.

'I thought you would have got over that by now.'

Jamilah emitted a strangled laugh. 'Got *over* it?' She crossed her fingers behind her back. 'I got over you long ago. I don't have anything to discuss with you—so, if you don't mind, my date will be looking for me.'

'He's no man for you. He's a runt—an obsequious

yes-man to the Sultan. What are you doing with him?'
Salman asked.

Jamilah was belligerent. 'What do you care? He's
perfect. The alpha male lost any fascination for me a
long time ago.'

She went to walk around Salman, but once again he
caught her arm. 'Tell me, do you shout out his name in
ecstasy?' he asked silkily. 'Do you rake his back with
your nails, pleading with him never to stop?'

He didn't have to say it, but the words hung between
them: *do you tell him you love him?* As if held back by
the flimsiest of walls, images and sensations flooded
Jamilah's body and mind. She was unaware of Salman
putting his hands on her arms and drawing her back in
front of him. Unaware of the intent in his dark gaze.
Unaware of the way his eyes dropped down her body,
and unaware of the guttural moan as he drew her into
him and his head lowered to hers.

She only became aware when the hot brand of his
mouth seared hers, plundering and demanding, forcing
her soft lips apart so that his tongue could snake out
between her small teeth and suck hers deep. Jamilah
had no defence. Desire burned up through her like a
living flame and hurled her into the fire.

It was shocking how well her body remembered his
touch—and how hungry she was for it. His hands on
her back felt so wonderful. Even more so when they
went lower and cupped her buttocks through the fine
silk of her dress. He pulled her up and into him, where
she could feel the hardening ridge of his desire, and
with a soft mewl of frustration she arched against him,
wanting more. Burning up with it. It was as if no time
had passed at all.

And all the while their mouths clung feverishly, as

if taking a first long drink of water from an oasis in the desert. It was only when Salman pulled her in even closer that an insidious image inserted itself—that of a red-haired woman being held in his arms, being made love to in exactly the same way.

Suddenly as cold as ice, Jamilah wrenched her head away and pulled free. She stood apart, aghast at how out of control she felt and how hard she was breathing.

'Stay away from me, Salman. There is nothing between us. *Nothing*. And there never was. You said it yourself. It was just a fling, and I'm not in the market for another one.'

She whirled around, her dark blue silk dress billowing about her as she stalked to the doors, praying he wouldn't stop her again. And then she turned back. 'You had your chance. You won't get another one. And for your information I've called out plenty of names in ecstasy since you, so don't think what happened just now was anything special.'

Salman watched Jamilah stalk back into the party and for a moment an almost unassailable wave of despair washed over him. Seeing her again had provoked a maelstrom of emotions within him—emotions he'd not felt since he'd last seen her. He sagged back against the wall, his legs suddenly weak as he registered how intoxicating it had been to kiss her, hold her in his arms.

How *familiar*. And how necessary it had been—as necessary as taking another breath. It was as if no time had passed. He wanted her with something close to desperation. On that thought he resolutely stood to his full height again. He'd already seduced her and then rejected her. He had no right to want her again. He never wanted women after he'd had them. So why should she be different?

His mouth was a grim line as he followed her back into the party. He hoped that she'd been telling the truth when she'd claimed those numerous lovers, because then it would mean that his impact on her had been minimal, and he could ignore the fact that he thought he'd seen vulnerability and hurt in those stunning blue eyes.

Jamilah knew her parting words to Salman had been a cheap shot, but they'd felt good for a moment—even if they weren't remotely true. Giving up any pretence of wanting to stay at the party, within an hour she had changed, her face scrubbed clean, and was in her Jeep and heading back to Merkazad.

Eventually she had to pull over on the hard shoulder of the motorway when tears blurred her vision too much. She rested her head on her hands on the steering wheel. She had to concede that she'd been hopelessly naïve in having thought she could remain unscathed after seeing Salman—and, worse, after *kissing* him, which she was sure had been nothing more than his cruel experiment to see how she still hungered for him.

On some level she'd never been able to believe how he'd turned into such a cruel and distant stranger that day.

She ruthlessly stopped her thoughts from deviating down a self-indulgent path where she'd try to find justification for Salman's behaviour. He was cold and heartless—he always had been. She'd just been too naïve to see it before.

She'd often speculated if the cataclysmic events that had once taken place in Merkazad had anything to do with Salman's insularity and darkness. Years before Merkazad had been invaded by an army from Al-Omar, which had been against its independence. Salman, his brother and their parents had been locked up in the bowels of the castle for three long months. It had been a difficult time for the whole country, and must have been traumatic for Nadim and Salman, but Jamilah had been just two at the time—far too young to remember the details.

Years after their liberation she'd always been the one allowed to spend time with Salman, when he hadn't even let his own brother or parents near. He'd never said much, but he'd listened to her inconsequential chatter—which had developed into tongue-tied embarrassment as she'd grown older. Yet he'd never made her feel uncomfortable. He'd even sought her out the day he left Merkazad for good. She'd been sixteen and hopelessly in love. He'd touched her cheek with a finger, such a wealth of bleakness in his eyes that she'd ached to comfort him, but he'd just said, 'See you around, kid.'

It was that bond that she believed had flared to life and blossomed over those three weeks in Paris. And yet if she believed what Salman had said to her there—and why wouldn't she?—it had all been a cruel illusion. She had to get it through her thick skull that there could be no justification for Salman's behaviour, and after tonight she *had* to draw a line under her obsession with him.

CHAPTER TWO

Present day.

SHEIKH SALMAN BIN KALID AL SAQR looked at the
shadows of the rotorblades of the helicopter as it flew
across the rocky expanse below him. They undulated
and snaked like dark ribbons over the mountaintops, and
when he looked further he could already see minarets
and the vague outlines of the buildings of Merkazad—
and the castle, where he was headed. His home and
birthplace. He was coming back for the first time in ten
years. Ten long years. And he felt numb inside.

He could remember the day he'd left, and the blistering argument he'd had with his older brother Nadim,
as if it had happened yesterday, despite every attempt
he'd made to block it out in the interim. They'd been
standing in Nadim's study, from where he'd been running the country since the tender age of twenty-one. His
older brother's responsibility had always struck fear into
Salman's heart because he'd known he would never have
been able to bear it.

Not because of a lack of ability, but because at the
age of eight he'd borne a horrific responsibility for his
own people that he'd never spoken about, and since that

time he'd cut Merkazad and everyone associated with it out of his heart.

As if to contradict him a memory rose up of Jamilah—the kinship he'd always felt with her, the way that for a long time she'd been the only person he could tolerate being near him and, in Paris, the ease with which he'd allowed her to seduce him to a softer place than he'd inhabited for as long as he could remember. *If ever.* And then the way he'd callously told her that it had been nothing, that she'd imagined them having some sort of bond. His skin prickled at being reminded of that now, and with ruthless efficiency he pushed it aside and focused on that moment with his brother again.

'This is your home, Salman!' his brother had shouted at him. 'I need you here with me. We need to rule together to be strong.'

Salman could remember how dead he'd felt inside, how removed from his brother's passion. He'd known that day would be his last in Merkazad. He was a free man. Since he'd been that eight-year-old boy, since the awful time of their incarceration, he'd felt aeons older than Nadim. 'Brother, this is your country now. Not mine. I will forge my own life. And I will not have you dictate to me. You have no right.'

He'd been able to see the struggle that had run through Nadim, and silently he'd sent out a dire warning: *don't even go there.* And as he'd watched he'd seen the fight leave Nadim. The weight of their history ran too deep between them. Salman felt bitter jealousy every time he looked at his brother and knew his integral goodness had never been compromised, or taken away, or violated. Salman's had when his childhood had been ripped away from him over a three-month period that had felt like three centuries.

Salman knew Nadim blamed himself for not protecting him all those years before. And even though Salman *knew* that it was irrational, because Nadim had been as helpless as he had, he still blamed Nadim for not saving him from the horrors he'd faced. In a way, he wanted his brother to feel that pain, and he inflicted it with impunity, knowing exactly what he was doing even while hating himself for it.

Blame, counter-blame and recrimination had festered between them for years, and it had only been last year, when Salman had seen Nadim at the Sultan of Al-Omar's birthday party, that he'd noticed a subtle change within himself. They'd spoken for mere tense moments, as was their custom when they met once or twice a year, but Salman had noticed a sense of weightlessness that he'd never felt before.

He grimaced, his eyes seeing but not seeing the vista of his own country unfold beneath him in all its rocky glory. The fact that he was flying over it right now, about to land in mere minutes, spoke volumes. A part of him still couldn't really believe that he was coming to Merkazad for a month in Nadim's stead, while he and his pregnant wife went to spend time in Ireland, where she came from, before they returned to have their first baby.

A ridiculous and archaic law said that if Merkazad was without its Sheikh for a month then a coup could be staged by the military to seat a new ruler. This law had been put in place at a time when they'd faced numerous and frequent attacks, to protect Merkazad from outside forces.

They'd been in this position only once before, when their parents had died and an interim governing body had been set up until Nadim had come of age. Luckily the army had been steadfastly loyal to their deceased father and to Nadim.

But Nadim had confided to Salman that since his marriage to Iseult some people were proving hard to win round, were disappointed that their Sheikh hadn't picked a Merkazadi woman to be his wife. He'd been concerned that until his heir was born their rule might be vulnerable for the first time in years. But if Salman was there in his place there would be no question of dissent.

Salman had found himself saying yes, bizarrely overriding his conscious intent to say no. He'd known on some deep level that one day he'd have to come home to face his demons, and it appeared the time had come. He'd put his completely incomprehensible decision down to that, and not to a latent sense of duty, or to passing time…or to the fact that since he'd seen Jamilah at that party a year ago he'd felt restless.

Even now he could remember the visceral kick in his chest when he'd turned in that corridor in the Hussein Palace and seen her standing before him like a vision, like something from a dream he'd never admitted having.

He'd only realised in that moment, as a kind of sigh of relief had gone through him, that in all the intervening years since Paris he'd gone to the Sultan's party every year hoping to see Jamilah…and he had not welcomed that revelation.

Salman's face darkened. She should have always been firmly off-limits—a woman he *should* have turned his back on—but he hadn't been able to resist. Even though he'd known that she'd been way, way too innocent for his cold heart he'd still seduced her in Paris, taken her innocence, proving to himself once again how debauched he really was.

And, not content with that, then he'd cruelly broken her heart. A bleakness filled his belly at remembering the pale set of her features that day. The incredible hurt in those beautiful eyes. He'd watched her innocence and joy turn into an adult's bitter disillusion right in front of him, even as he'd been telling himself that he was doing her a favour.

He reassured himself that he'd saved her—from him and other men like him. Because he himself was beyond saving. He'd seen the face of evil and that would taint him for ever, and anyone around him, which was why he never allowed anyone too close.

Yet all that knowledge hadn't stopped him from kissing Jamilah at the Sultan's party. He'd only had to imagine her with that ineffectual date of hers and he'd been overcome with a dark desire to stamp her, brand her as his. His body throbbed to life now, making him shift uncomfortably; she'd tasted as sweetly sensuous as she had when he'd first kissed her in Paris, when he'd known he was doing the wrong thing but had been overcome with a lust so intense it had made him dizzy.

With an effort he forced his mind away from the disturbing fact that in the past year no woman had managed to arouse his once insatiable libido. But merely thinking of Jamilah now was doing just that, as if to taunt him, because she was the last woman he could ever touch again. If he had any chance of redeeming a tiny morsel of his soul it would be in this.

Salman knew Nadim suspected something had happened between them, and of course he didn't approve. The protective warning had been implicit in Nadim's voice in their last conversation. 'You're unlikely to see much of Jamilah. She lives and works down at the stables, and is extremely busy with her work there.' And that, Salman told himself now, suited him just fine—because the mere thought of even seeing a horse or the stables sent clammy chills of dread across his skin. He wouldn't be making a visit there any time soon.

With that thought lingering as the helicopter started to descend over the lush watered Merkazadi castle grounds, reality hit Salman, and claustrophobia surged along with panic. He fought the urge to tell the pilot to turn around. He was strong enough to withstand a month in his own country. He had to be. He'd heard far worse stories than his; he'd been humbled over and over again. He owed it to those who had trusted him with their stories to face this.

Not for the first time in his life did he wish that he could resort to the easy way out of drugs and alcohol.

He sighed deeply as the distinctive white castle came into clear view, the ornate latticed walls and flat-roofed terraces all at once achingly familiar and rousing a veritable flood of memories, some terrifying. He would get through this as he'd got through his life up to this point—by distracting himself from the pain.

'Miss Jamilah—he stumbled out of the helicopter with his shirt half undone and torn jeans. He looked like a…a rock star, not the second in line to rule Merkazad.' The main housekeeper screwed up her wizened face and spat out disgustedly, 'He is nothing like his brother. He is a disgrace to—'

'Hana, that's enough.' They were in a meeting to discuss the domestic schedule of the castle while Nadim and Iseult were away, and Jamilah was having a hard enough time just functioning since she'd heard Salman's arrival in the helicopter the previous day.

The older woman flushed brick-red. 'I'm sorry, Miss Jamilah. I forgot myself for a moment…'

Jamilah smiled tightly. 'It's fine. Don't worry. Look, he's only here till Nadim and Iseult get back…and then everything will be back to normal.'

Yeah, right.

The housekeeper's face lit up. 'And next year we will have a new baby in the castle!'

Jamilah let her prattle on excitedly, and hoped the dart of hurt she felt lance her wasn't apparent on her face or in her eyes. She loved Nadim, and she loved Iseult, who had become a very close friend, but much to her ongoing shame she couldn't help but feel a little jealous of their exuberant happiness.

In truth, when Nadim had told her they would be going to Ireland to see Iseult's family while they still had time before the birth, Jamilah had felt a tinge of relief. To bear witness to their intense love and absorption every day was becoming more and more difficult. And it had only intensified with news of Iseult's pregnancy some six months previously. Nadim hardly let Iseult out of his sight, and cosseted her like a prize jewel. Jamilah knew it drove Iseult crazy, but then she was as bad he was—visibly pining for her husband if he was away from her side for more than an hour.

Jamilah's relief that she would have some respite had been spectacularly eclipsed when Nadim had casually mentioned over dinner that Salman would be taking over as acting ruler while they were gone.

She'd not missed the way Nadim and Iseult had looked at her intently for her reaction; they hadn't asked questions after her bizarre behaviour at the Sultan's party last year, but it had been obvious it had something to do with Salman.

She was proud of the way she'd absorbed the shock into her body and kept on sipping her wine, willing her hands not to show a tremor. She'd said nonchalantly, 'That's nice. It's been so long since he came home...'

Nadim had said gently, 'You could go to France, if you like. Check up on the stables there?'

Jamilah had tensed all over and sat up straight. *'No.'* She was aghast that they might think she would crumble, or that she would let Salman's presence affect her work. She'd shaken her head and sealed her fate. 'Not at all. I won't be going anywhere. We're far too busy here...'

But now, when Hana stood up and asked, 'Will you come to the castle to talk to the staff?' Jamilah almost shouted out another visceral *no,* and had to calm herself.

She smiled and said, as breezily as she could, shamelessly playing to Hana's pride, 'Why would I need to come to the castle when you have it all in hand so beautifully? We're busy here at the stables with some new arrivals...you can call me if anything comes up.'

To her intense relief Hana didn't argue, and left. Jamilah sank back into her office chair, feeling as edgy as a new colt, her heart racing.

A month.

One whole month of avoiding going anywhere near the castle and Salman. At least here at the stables where she lived she was relatively safe. For as long as she'd known him he'd had an abhorrence of horses, so she knew he wouldn't come near them.

She was over him, so the fact that he was right now less than ten minutes away meant nothing to her. Nothing at all.

* * *

Jamilah's phone rang at five-thirty a.m.—just as she was about to go out and do her morning round of the stables to check everyone was where they should be. She was grouchy from lack of sleep and the constant feeling of being on edge. And for the past few days there had been the non-stop clatter of helicopter rotorblades, as numerous choppers took off and landed in the castle's grounds. Even though it was a fair distance to the stables, some had flown close enough to the horses to spook them for hours. Jamilah had heard through the robust grapevine that Salman was hosting an unending series of parties at the castle.

Now she gritted her teeth and answered the phone in the office, which was part of her private rooms. All she heard on the other end was hysterical sobbing, until finally she managed to calm Hana down enough to listen for a minute.

With an icy cold anger rising, she eventually bit out, through a break in the tirade, 'I'm on my way.'

Clinging on to that cold rage, to distract her from the prospect of seeing Salman again, Jamilah went outside and got into her Jeep, making the ten-minute journey to the castle courtyard in five minutes, where Hana was wringing her hands.

As soon as Jamilah stepped out of her Jeep Hana was babbling. *'All night, every night…such loud music— and the food! It's too much…couldn't keep up with the demands and then they started throwing things…in the ceremonial ballroom! If Nadim was here…'*

Gently but firmly Jamilah cut through Hana's hysterics. 'Get the staff organised for a clean-up, and get Sakmal here with a coach. I'll have all these guests out of here this morning.'

By the time Jamilah had reached the quarters Salman

had commandeered for his private use about an hour later her rage was no longer icy but boiling over. She'd just seen the devastation caused by what appeared to be half of Europe's Eurotrash party brigade, and she'd just supervised about fifty seriously disgruntled, still inebriated people onto a coach, from where they would be delivered into Al-Omar and back home.

She pushed open the door to Salman's suite and slammed it back against a wall. The immediate dart of hurt at what she saw nearly made her double over, and that made her rage burn even brighter. At the evidence that he was still affecting her.

Two bodies were sprawled on an ornately brocaded couch. An empty champagne bottle and glasses were strewn around them. The nubile blonde woman was caked in make-up, wearing a tiny sparkly, spangly dress. She looked up drunkenly from where she lay beside a sleeping Salman, one arm flung across his bare and tautly muscled chest. Thankfully he was at least wearing jeans.

'Excuse me,' she slurred in cut-glass tones, 'who do you think you are?'

Jamilah strode over, trying to block out the sensually indolent olive-skinned body of Salman, and took the woman's skinny arm, hauling her up.

'Ow!'

Jamilah was unrepentant as she marched the sluggish woman over to where two maids hovered anxiously at the door, clad head to toe in black, their huge brown eyes growing wider and wider. Jamilah said with icy disdain, 'Girls, please escort this guest to the coach, after she's picked up her things, and then tell Sakmal he can go. That should be everyone.'

Jamilah shut the door firmly on the woman's drunken

protestations and sighed deeply. She turned round and Salman hadn't budged an inch. Her heart clenched painfully; he'd always slept like the dead, and now that was obviously exacerbated by his alcohol intake. Her eyes roved over his hard-hewn muscle-packed form. She hated to admit it, but for an indolent, louche playboy he possessed the body of an athlete in his prime.

Dark stubble shadowed his firm jaw, and a lock of black hair had fallen over his forehead, making him look deceptively innocent. Long black lashes caressed those ridiculously sculpted cheekbones. He looked like a dark fallen angel who might have literally just dropped out of the sky.

But an angel, fallen or otherwise, he most certainly was *not*.

Jamilah clenched her jaw, as if that could counteract the treacherous rising of heat within her, and went to the bathroom where she found what she was looking for. Coming back into the main drawing room, she said a mental prayer for forgiveness to Nadim and Hana for the damage she was about to do to the soft furnishings, and then she threw the entire bucket of icy cold water over Salman.

Salman thought he was being attacked. Reflexes that had been honed long, long ago snapped into action, and he was on his feet and tense before he really knew what was happening.

In seconds, though, he had assessed the situation and forced locked muscles to relax. Jamilah was standing in front of him with an empty bucket and a belligerent look on her beautiful face, and something inside him rose up with an almost giddy surge. For the first time since he'd returned he felt centred—not rudderless and scarily close to the edge of his control.

With her hair tied back, no make-up, dressed in a white shirt, jeans and riding boots, she might have passed for eighteen. Her stunning blue eyes were glittering like bright sapphires, and a line of pink slashed each cheek with colour. She was a veritable jewel of beauty compared to the artificially enhanced women who'd been vying for his attention these last few days, and self-disgust curled inside him when he remembered the one who'd eventually fallen into a drunken slumber beside him earlier that morning.

He'd vowed to order his private jet and get rid of the horde of unwanted guests, realising what a mistake he'd made, but it would appear by the look on Jamilah's face that it had already been taken care of.

'How dare you?' Jamilah was saying now, in a suspiciously quivery voice which he guessed had more to do with anger than emotion. 'How *dare* you come back here and proceed to turn this castle into your personal playground? Poor Hana is distraught. She has quite enough to be doing without pandering to you and all the Little Lord Fauntleroys you invited to join in the fun. And apart from the chaos and destruction here, your *friends'* constant arrival by helicopter has been spooking the horses at the stables.'

Energy crackled between them.

Salman rocked back on his heels and surveyed Jamilah with a lazy sweep, up and down. He seemed to be oblivious to the fact that he was soaking wet, and with a gulp Jamilah could see that this was not proceeding the way she'd expected at all. Salman didn't look remotely contrite, or even drunk. His eyes were as sharp as ever. And on *her.* She had to consciously not let her gaze drop to where his jeans must be plastered against his crotch and thighs.

He crossed his arms nonchalantly across his chest, making his biceps bulge, and Jamilah had the very belated realisation that she'd just wakened a sleeping panther. He drawled, 'Not even a kiss hello to greet me? That's not very nice, now, is it?'

Jamilah put the bucket down because she was afraid she'd drop it. She stood up to see Salman staring at her with a disturbing glint in his eye. Feeling the sudden urge to escape, and fast, she said glacially, 'Clearly you feel that Merkazad is too boring to sustain your attention. I'd suggest that if you're looking for entertainment you should follow your friends to B'harani, where they're headed right now on a tour bus.'

For a second Jamilah could have sworn she saw the merest smile touch Salman's lips, but then it was gone. And the urge to escape grew more acute. She whirled round to leave the room, but before she could reach the door she was whirled back again by a strong hand gripping her arm and a guttural, 'Where do you think you're going?'

'What the—?' she spluttered ineffectually.

Salman knew he should be letting Jamilah go. He'd *told* himself that he would not pursue her. But faced with her now, her timeless beauty, that sleek curvaceous body, he knew it was too much for his battered soul to resist.

Salman arched one ebony brow. 'Like I said, can't you even greet me with a civil hello?'

Jamilah glared up at him, already cursing herself for having come here to deal with this. 'Why would I want to bother saying hello to someone who can't even treat his own home or staff with any respect?'

His eyes flashed blackly. 'Exactly. This is my home, and you would do well to remember that.'

Jamilah spat out, 'You mean remember my *place?* Is that it, Salman? It's been a long time since anyone had to remind me that I'm not part of your family.'

She tried to break free, but his grip was too strong, and then two hands drew her round in front of him, and his gaze fairly blistered down into her defiant one. Of course she wasn't a member of their family; for all of Nadim's care, inclusion and protection after her parents had died Jamilah had always known her place—so why was she provoking Salman like this now?

'That's not what I meant at all, and you know it. The fact is that this is my home and I shall do as I like here. As acting ruler I don't have to answer to anyone.'

Jamilah stuck her chin out pugnaciously, something deep and visceral goading her on. 'You'll answer to *me.* I may not be the ruler, but the staff here know who is in charge and it's not you. You need to earn their respect first. And I won't stand by and watch you come in here and desecrate Nadim and Iseult's home.'

Before Jamilah could even question where that urge to provoke had come from suddenly they were a lot closer, and her breath faltered as Salman's unique and intensely male scent washed over her. Dimly she recognised that she couldn't smell drink on his breath. He hadn't been drunk? That didn't fit with the scene she'd just witnessed.

'Like I said—' his voice was as glacial as hers '—this is my home as much as it is Nadim's, and I will invite whomever I want, whenever I want.'

Unable to articulate a response, and quickly becoming overwhelmed by Salman's intoxicating proximity,

Jamilah tried to break free of his hold again, twisting around in his hands.

All it did, though, was force her back into his hard chest—and then she heard a muttered curse. Suddenly strong arms were below her breasts, and she was being lifted clear off her feet and carried bodily towards the bathroom. She kicked out with her legs, but her struggles were futile and puny in the face of Salman's overpowering strength. She was plastered against a hard, *wet* body. And that was entirely her fault.

She couldn't even get a word out before they were in the bathroom, and Salman easily held her with one arm while he turned on the shower. Both her hands were trying to free herself, to no avail. His arm was like a steel bar. She could feel her hair loosening from its untidy ponytail.

The water was running, and steam had started to rise around them when she finally spluttered out, 'What the *hell* do you think you are doing? Let me down this instant!'

In that moment Salman walked them both under the warm spray of the huge shower, and she heard him say grimly over her head, 'Giving you a little taste of your own medicine, Miss High-and-mighty.'

CHAPTER THREE

THE inarticulate rage that had risen up within Salman seconds ago was already diminishing, and he knew it had had more to do with this woman's effect on him than her belligerence and anger. And now he couldn't see anything but Jamilah, her clothes already soaked through and sticking to that glorious body.

Jamilah was gasping in shock, her back against the wall of the shower. Water was streaming over her head, face, into her eyes, and Salman's hand was splayed across her abdomen, holding her in place. Through the steam she could see his glittering obsidian gaze, his hair plastered to his skull, and water sluicing down that powerful chest, through the dark smattering of hair, over his blunt nipples.

She tried to smack his hand away, but he merely put it back and said grimly, 'You're not going anywhere.'

Humiliation scorched up through Jamilah as she became very aware of how drenched she was, and how her clothes were plastered to her body. As if reading her thoughts, Salman dropped his eyes, and she could feel her breasts respond, growing heavy, her nipples peaking almost painfully against her wet bra and shirt. She could only imagine how see-through the flimsy material must be under the powerful spray. A flash of fire lit his eyes, and they went darker in an instant—and, *awfully,* she felt an answering rush of heat.

Once again she tried to get free, but Salman merely moved closer and took her hands, raising them above her head. She struggled in earnest now, feeling intensely vulnerable, but it was a struggle against the fire that was gathering pace inside her body, in her blood. She had to stop abruptly when her hips came into explosive contact with his.

'Let me go.'

She longed to go for his vulnerable area with a knee, but he quickly manoeuvred them so that he could thrust a thigh between her legs and shook his head, saying, 'Ah-ah...'

The shock of feeling that powerful thigh between hers rendered her mute. All too easily he held her two hands in one of his, like an iron manacle. His other hand drifted down to cup her jaw and turn her face up to his. The spray bounced off him, cocooning them in steam. She gritted her jaw and tried to turn away, but he ruthlessly turned her head back.

He smiled down at her, and it was the smile of a dangerous predator. 'Aren't you even a little bit glad to see me?'

A treacherous kick of her heart made Jamilah all but spit at him. 'You're the last person I'd be happy to see, Salman al Saqr.'

He shook his head mock-mournfully and tutted. 'All those strong feelings still under the surface, Jamilah?'

Cold horror snaked through her, despite the heat around them. She had to protect herself. She forced her body to relax and mirrored his own easy demeanour. She even smiled sweetly. 'On the contrary. I don't have feelings for you, Salman. I never did. Whatever you saw in Paris was a very transitory and misplaced affection for a first lover. That's all. You mean nothing to me. I am merely angry because you disrespect your brother and sister-in-law, who I care about greatly, and your home. You've caused chaos in the castle, and I refuse to stand by and watch it for a moment longer.'

Salman's gaze glittered down. His jaw clenched. It was getting harder to keep her body relaxed as he came even closer and she felt his hips grind into hers. And then it was all but impossible when she felt the thrillingly hard evidence of his arousal. Heat climbed upwards and she lashed out. 'You're an animal.'

Salman growled, 'I agree. I feel very animalistic at the moment.' His eyes had grown heavy and dangerously slumberous, but still with that provocative fire igniting in their depths.

He tightened his hold on her jaw and swooped down, his mouth a searing brand over hers before she could take another breath. Their bodies touched, chest to chest, hip to hip, and Jamilah felt an immediate wild excitement coursing through her blood.

She wanted to rip the wet clothes from her body and arch closer to Salman, to feel wet skin on wet skin. A vivid memory of another shower, another time, flared up. He had lifted her naked body against the wall and urged her to wrap her legs around his waist. He'd found the hot wet core of her and had surged up and into her, making everything blur into a heat haze of passion.

Anger at her reaction and at the vividness of the memory made her kiss him back, defiantly at first, and then she realised the folly of that when Salman pulled her in even closer. She had to battle harder than she'd ever done in her life not to respond, not to let him suck her under to a dark vortex where past and present might merge and make her forget where she was and what he had done to her.

She seized her opportunity when he lifted his head momentarily. With an abrupt move she snaked out from under him and out of the shower, dripping water everywhere and only then realising how much the wall had been supporting her when her legs felt like jelly.

Salman turned slowly under the spray of water and looked at her. She fought the wild clamour of her pulse. As she watched his hand snaked down to his jeans. He flipped open the top button and drawled, 'I'm going to make myself more comfortable, if you'd care to do the same and join me?'

Jamilah dragged her gaze back up and shook her head, feeling as if she were on fire inside. 'I wouldn't join you if we were the two last humans on earth and the future of civilisation depended on us procreating.'

Salman smiled and lazily pulled down his zip. Jamilah could see the whorls of dark hair which led to his sex in her peripheral vision. Heat threatened to engulf her completely. She wondered why she couldn't move.

And then Salman said, 'But wouldn't we make beautiful babies?'

Jamilah made a garbled sound. She was so mad she wanted to cry, or slap Salman's mocking face. And through that emotion, completely unbidden, came the sudden *awful* yearning to be heavy with this man's child. That brought with it the return of bitter reality and the sharpest pain of all—because she *knew* what it had felt like to carry this man's child for the briefest time, before nature had taken its tragic course. She could still feel that dragging pain, the wrenching sense of loss, and he would never know.

Even now he was still mocking, taunting, pulling his wet jeans down over lean hips and off, blissfully unaware of the nuclear implosion happening within Jamilah. Before he could see any of it she tore her gaze away and grabbed a towel hanging on a nearby rail. While she still could, she walked on wobbly legs out of the bathroom to the sound of a dark, mocking chuckle and a softly intoned, *'Coward.'*

Salman stood in the shower after Jamilah had walked out, his hands against the wall and his head downbent between them. Only minutes before he'd held her captive. Dripping wet and the sexiest thing he'd ever seen. He finally turned the water to cold as he faced the prospect that for the first time since his teens he might be forced to pleasure himself just to reclaim some sanity. But he had to acknowledge now that his sanity had fled along with Jamilah.

Her white shirt had turned see-through the minute the water had hit, clearly showing her white lace bra and the puckered tips of her berry-brown nipples. Her breasts were still beautifully round, firm and high. And he knew that they would fill his palms like succulent fruits.

He groaned softly when his wayward body persisted in responding, despite the stinging cold spray, and he valiantly resisted the urge to wrap his hand around himself and seek all too transitory relief. There was only one way to relief now. Past or no past, history be damned, one thing was clear: he *would* have Jamilah back in his bed until he'd sated himself—until he'd sated them both. Because their desire was mutual, explosive and unfinished. And there was no way he could survive a month here without taking her. He'd go crazy.

All concerns for Jamilah's emotional welfare and the state of his soul were dissolving in a wave of heat. He took some reassurance from the way she'd stood up to him. He could be in no doubt that she was no longer some shy, timid and idealistic virgin. *And you did that to her.* He blocked out the voice.

His mind stalled for a moment. *Dammit,* she had been a virgin. He'd assumed that she'd been at least a little bit experienced. He could still remember his shock when he'd thrust into that slick tightness and felt her momentary hesitation, seen the fleeting pain on her face. And then heard her husky moans and pleas for him to keep going. She'd just been too seductive. He was only human, and he hadn't been able to stop.

His mouth tightened. But hadn't she all but told him that she'd had plenty of other lovers, and that the turmoil he'd witnessed that day in Paris had merely been a passing crush on her first lover. He should feel comforted by that thought...yet he didn't.

With an abrupt move he switched off the shower and stepped out. Towelling himself dry roughly, he made a mental vow that if he was consigning himself to hell for ever by resolving to have Jamilah in his bed, then she was coming with him—all the way.

As he found and dragged on clean clothes he thrust thoughts of Jamilah aside with effort. He had some things to attend to—and one of them was making sure that his ill-advised party guests had indeed been shown the door. For the first time in years living vicariously through those around him, watching them lose all sense of self and envying them their opiate nirvana, hadn't worked to block out his own reality.

* * *

'I apologised to Hana, and to Hisham.'

Jamilah steeled herself before she turned from where she'd been unpacking her suitcase in one of the guest suites. She hadn't wanted Salman to know so soon that she'd given in to both Hana's, and Nadim's chief aide's pleas for her to move up to the castle. Taking a deep breath, she finally did turn round—to see Salman in dark trousers and a white shirt, leaning insouciantly against the open door.

'I know,' she said stiffly, trying to ignore the response in her body and treacherously wishing she wasn't wearing her habitual uniform of jeans and a shirt—albeit fresh ones. It had been a long day since that eventful morning, and she was exhausted.

She didn't need to be reminded of how he'd wound the intractable Hana around his little finger. She'd been all but blushing when she'd told Jamilah of his *apparent* heartfelt apology.

'So…' Salman quirked a brow. 'You've been sent to babysit me? Are you going to ground me for bad behaviour?'

Jamilah heard the edge to his voice and guessed that he didn't often find himself in the position of having to apologise for his actions. She didn't feel that he was in any way repentant, despite his apology.

She focused on his eyes, and then wished she could look anywhere else when she was sucked into the dark depths and butterflies erupted in her stomach. Salman had a unique ability to plug into her deepest emotions and stir them around. He'd *always* had that ability.

That realisation made her voice frigid. 'They asked me to come and stay here. That's all. With Nadim and Iseult away there's a lot to take care of, and clearly you're not interested in taking responsibility.'

She saw his eyes flash at that, but it was gone in an instant and Jamilah wondered why she should be feeling bad.

Salman's mouth twisted into a mocking smile. 'What? And not live up to my reputation as the prodigal bad-boy brother?'

Jamilah's own lush mouth firmed. 'Something like that.' And then, before she could stop herself, she asked curiously, 'Why *did* you come home?'

A dangerous glint came into Salman's eye. 'I'll tell you if you have dinner with me tonight.'

He was flirting with her.

Jamilah's belly tightened in rejection of that even as a rush of heat washed through her body. She firmed her jaw. 'Just because your odious friends have gone, I am not available to entertain you in their absence.'

She stalked over to the door and started to close it purposefully, uncaring of the fact that Salman was in the way. To her abject relief he stepped back. But just before she could close it he stopped it with a hand and said, 'I'm going to be here for a few weeks, Jamilah… you won't be able to avoid me for ever. Especially not now that we're going to be under the same roof.'

Jamilah snorted indelicately. 'This castle is big enough for an army. We won't have to make much of an effort to stay out of each other's way, Salman. And, believe me, I have no intention of seeking you out. Now, if you'll excuse me, I've had a long day, I'm tired, and I want to go to bed.'

Much to her chagrin, she still couldn't close the door. She glared up at Salman and tried not to notice that he'd shaved. His jaw was dark and smooth. His clean and intensely masculine scent teased her nostrils. He was one of the few men she knew who hadn't ever worn overpowering cologne.

'This isn't it, Jamilah, not by a long shot. We have unfinished business.'

Fear caught Jamilah's insides into a knot. She knew she simply would not be able to survive if Salman decided he wanted to seduce her again just because he was bored, or curious. 'We finished any business we had a long time ago, Salman, and the sooner you realise that the better. And, quite frankly, I don't care if this is your home and you're the acting ruler—just stay out of my way.'

When Salman stood on the balcony of his suite a short while later, he felt a hardness enter his belly. The view of Merkazad at night was spread below him. It was a small city but beautiful, full of soaring floodlit minarets and ancient buildings nestling alongside more modern architecture. When he'd been much younger, before the rebel invasion, he'd loved to watch it at night and dream of all sorts of fantastical tales, and the great wide world beyond…but then, during and after the incarceration, it had become a prison to be escaped at all costs…

He was waiting for the inevitable rise of emotion, for nausea to cripple him as it had done whenever he'd looked at this view before. But emotion wasn't rising in its usual unassailable wave. Instead he felt suspiciously calm. As if something had shifted and this view was no longer as malevolently threatening as it had been for years.

All he could think about was Jamilah and how beautiful she'd looked just now, with that fall of silky midnight-black hair in a curtain around her shoulders and down her back. His gut clenched. She had looked tired. Faint purple shadows under her huge blue eyes. And that vulnerability had made him want to gather her up into his arms and carry her somewhere far away, into the dark starlit night, and lay her down underneath him. He amended his impulse. He just *wanted* her. He didn't want to protect her.

But he had once… He'd been twelve and she'd been just six when she'd broken through the numbness encasing him to provoke a protective instinct. He could remember the moment by their parents' graves as clearly as if it were yesterday. She'd been so still, so stoic. He'd felt an affinity with her that he hadn't felt with anyone else.

The earth shifted ominously beneath his feet as he had to acknowledge that perhaps Jamilah could be the key to his unfamiliar feeling of equanimity. That thought disturbed him far more than any view could.

Two nights later, as Jamilah lay in bed unable to sleep, she had to admit to herself that she probably would be better off if she was seeing Salman every day. Perhaps it would inure her to his presence? A voice laughed mockingly in her head at that. But anything had to be better than this awful restless *hot* feeling. She was useless at work, jumping at the slightest sound. She was turning into a nervous wreck.

She'd heard people talking and speculating about him—especially the younger girls at the stables. *'Is it true he's more wealthy than even Sheikh Nadim?' 'He's the most handsome man I've ever seen, but why doesn't he come to the stables?'*

This last comment had been made dreamily by one of the girls who'd run an errand to the castle. Before Jamilah could say anything, her chief aide, a man called

Abdul, had said curtly, 'He is the Sheikh. And he can do as he wishes. Now get back to work.'

Jamilah had looked at him aghast. Abdul was the most mild-mannered man she'd ever known, and had worked at the stables for longer than anyone could remember. He rarely opened his mouth to anyone. The girls had scuttled off, and he'd immediately apologised to Jamilah red-faced, clearly mortified. She'd waved off his apology, not knowing where the sudden passion had blazed from, and with the curious feeling that he'd been defending Salman. But from what?

With a groan of frustration, mixed with anger at her obsessive thoughts about Salman, Jamilah threw back the covers and got out of bed. She stripped off and went straight to her shower, where she endured the icy spray until her teeth were chattering—as if she could numb all feeling.

'You will have dinner with me tonight.'

Salman's voice was an autocratic decree from the ruler of Merkazad. If it had been Nadim, Jamilah would have said yes immediately. But it was Salman, and as her suddenly sweaty hand gripped the handset of the phone in her office she said waspishly, 'Why should I?'

Salman sighed, and her skin prickled.

'Because we need to discuss some things…'

Her heart thumped. 'I have nothing to discuss with you.'

Salman said, with an edge to his voice, 'What you said to me the other day appears to be true. As much as I might be acting ruler, I'm being constantly diverted to you.'

Jamilah couldn't even feel a bit smug for a second.

She just said faintly, 'I told you you'd need to earn their respect.'

'And until that day dawns I'm afraid that I need you—'

Jamilah's mind blanked when he said those words, and she had to concentrate just to keep up.

'To have dinner with me and discuss official business. Or do you want me to bother Nadim and his pregnant wife while they are spending time with her family?'

Immediately Jamilah answered, because she knew Salman would have no compunction about disturbing them, 'No. Of course not.' She continued in a rush, before she could lose her nerve, 'I'm finished at work by seven. I'll see you at eight.'

Salman's voice was husky. 'Good. I'll be looking forward to it, Jamilah.'

Jamilah let the phone drop with a clatter and put hands to hot cheeks. Suddenly breathless, she had to consciously block out evocative images and memories of those weeks in Paris and tell herself that never again would she be so foolish as to let Salman anywhere near the vulnerable heart of her.

A few hours later, though, seated in Nadim's private formal suite, which Salman had moved into, at an intimate dining table, Jamilah was struggling hard to cling on to her sense of equilibrium. Salman sat opposite her in a black shirt. It made him look even darker, more dangerous. She took another sip of delicious red wine and cursed the impulse which had made her change into a black dress and high-heeled shoes. And leave her hair down. And put on the slightest touch of mascara. She told herself it was just armour. And she needed all the armour she could get.

Salman put down his knife and fork and sat back, wiping his mouth with a napkin. She'd once teased him about the single-minded way he ate. To block the insidious memory, she commented, 'You're not drinking…' And then she smiled sweetly. 'Still recovering from last week? They say it gets harder with age to cope with the after-effects.'

Almost curtly Salman said, 'I don't drink.'

Jamilah frowned, and Salman's whole body tightened. If she had any idea how aroused and hot he was for her right now she'd run a mile. Since Hisham had shown her in earlier he'd been in a state of heat and lust. He'd expected her to be in jeans and a shirt, and wouldn't have been surprised to see mucky riding boots.

But she was dressed in something floaty and black. And, while it revealed nothing overt, it clung to her soft bountiful curves with a loving touch. All he wanted to do was smash aside the table between them and rip it off her.

He forced an urbane smile and tried to clamp down on his recently dormant but now raging libido. 'And I don't do drugs, either.'

Jamilah was reminded of how he'd certainly appeared sober enough the morning she'd found him passed out. His admission made her feel funny…curious. She shook her head, not understanding. 'How could you bear to be around those people, then? How could you invite them here and let them run amok like that?'

Salman smiled, but it didn't reach his eyes. 'What can I say? I'm drawn to their instinctive hedonism. I find their lack of engagement with reality fascinating.'

Jamilah had the sudden inexplicable sense that he *envied* those people, and battled her growing curiosity. Her voice was scathing. 'I find that hard to believe. It would be impossible to stay in any kind of proximity to that kind of world without being out of your head.'

His eyes darkened to unreadable black. 'Believe it or not, I've been drunk once, and only once.'

At that admission, which Jamilah could see he didn't welcome, his face shut down, became impassive. Jamilah remembered then that Salman had never drunk to excess during the time she'd been with him.

And then he said, 'What about you, Jamilah? Are you such a paragon of virtue that you've never over-indulged?'

Jamilah's insides contracted. She could remember heady nights of wine and food when she'd been with Salman, the delicious tipsiness that had imbued her and Paris with a magical hue of romance. It certainly hadn't done the same for Salman. Almost unconsciously she pushed away her half-full glass and answered, 'I'm no paragon of virtue, Salman, but, no, I don't feel that I need to see life through a veil of inebriation and crippling hangovers.'

He smiled mockingly, and she couldn't fail to notice something unbearably bleak this time. 'Because you wake up each morning with a sense of optimism about your life and the future?'

Jamilah went still inside. Once she'd been like that. So long ago that she almost couldn't remember it. But she couldn't deny that now every day when she woke up there was a dull sense of loss…of emptiness. He didn't know that losing the baby had made her fearful that she might never get pregnant again. No one knew what she'd been through. And she wasn't about to bare her soul to Salman now.

Much as she hated to admit it, her sense of isolation

had been heightened recently by Nadim and Iseult's unabashed joy in finding each other.

She wiped at her mouth perfunctorily with a napkin and sat up straight, looking pointedly at her watch even if she didn't register the time. 'What did you want to discuss, Salman? I've got an early start in the morning. We've got three new colts that need to be broken in.'

She looked at him then, and was taken aback at the sudden ashen tinge to his skin. Instinctively she leant forward and said, 'Salman?'

But, as if she'd imagined it, he recovered. He stood up abruptly and walked over to a cabinet, where he took out some papers. Jamilah felt decidedly shaky, and tried not to let her eyes dwell on his tight buttocks encased in superbly cut black trousers. He turned and came back and her face flamed guiltily. She willed down the heat, hating feeling so out of control.

He put down the sheaf of documents and she picked up the top one, feeling at a serious disadvantage as he stood looming over her with hands in his pockets. She could see that it was a press communiqué about an important series of meetings of Middle Eastern heads of state to be held in Paris later that week, regarding the global financial crisis.

She looked up at him blankly. 'So? What am I supposed to be seeing here?'

'I have to go to Paris in Nadim's place.'

Feeling threatened, and not sure why, and also more than a little disturbed by the fact that she wasn't feeling relief at being informed of Salman's incipient departure, she stood up and said, 'Well, have a good trip. I'll try not to miss you too much.'

She realised then that Salman hadn't moved back, and now they were almost touching. With a spurt of panic

Jamilah moved, but her heel caught in the luxurious carpet and she felt herself pitching backwards. At her helpless cry, two big hands came around her waist and hauled her up again. Breathing heavily, from fright and unwanted sensation, Jamilah could only look up into the black pools of Salman's eyes.

His fingers tightened on her waist and he said ominously, 'You're coming to Paris with me.'

CHAPTER FOUR

It took a few seconds for his words to sink in, and then Jamilah started to struggle. Her hands were on his arms, and the feel of his bunched muscles was scrambling nearly every thought. Even so, she managed to get out, 'No way.'

The thought of going anywhere with this man, much less back to *Paris*, had cold, clammy horror sinking into her bones. He wasn't releasing her, and Jamilah stopped struggling. It was futile.

She asserted stiffly, 'I'm needed here.'

To her utter relief Salman released her then, and she took a hurried but careful step back. He lifted up another piece of paper and showed it to her. 'I think you'll find that a copy of this is probably in your office, too.'

Jamilah took it and read, the words swimming before her eyes. She saw that it was from Nadim.

Jamilah should go with you. There are going to be some important people there from the biggest stables in Dubai, and I've already set up some meetings. Unfortunately the meeting in Paris coincides with the annual yearling sales here in Ireland, otherwise I'd go myself...

She looked up, and dropped the piece of paper to the table before Salman could see her hand start to shake. How could Nadim do this to her? And then she answered herself bitterly—because she'd put on a great show of making them believe that she cared nothing for the fact that Salman was going to be in Merkazad. And this was no more of a request than Nadim had made of her in the past. It was quite usual for her to go to meetings like this if he was otherwise occupied. After all, she did run the Merkazad stables.

She looked at Salman in shock, something else occurring to her. 'But it'll be a disaster if you go. Are you planning on going to any of the meetings with the leaders?' Before he could answer she said, 'Do you know how much damage you could do to Merkazad and Nadim if you insult a leader at something like this?'

She saw something unfathomable cross Salman's face. For a moment it looked like *pride*. As if she'd injured his pride. His jaw clenched. He smiled, and it was hard, harder than she'd ever seen. 'Which is precisely why you should come with me. You don't want to have a loose cannon wrecking Merkazad's reputation, do you?'

He was mocking her. She knew that. And she knew she deserved it. Even though she didn't believe he could be trusted with such a responsibility. This, after all, was the man who had left the running of his country squarely on the shoulders of his brother for as long as she could remember. Even when they'd been teenagers, and they had been home for the holidays, Salman had regularly eschewed the lengthy lessons in Merkazadi rule and law that Nadim had had to endure in preparation for his role. And yet, for reasons unknown to her, Nadim had never called him on it.

The tension between the two brothers had always been palpable, and Jamilah was aware that this was the first time Salman appeared to be softening in some respect—taking an interest even if it was somewhat forced and clearly unwelcome. Did she want to be the person who sabotaged that?

If she was to make a fuss and insist on staying in Merkazad she'd merely be proving to Salman that to her the thought of returning to Paris with him equated to a minor mental breakdown. Her one saving grace at the moment was that he believed her to be over their brief liaison.

She came to a reluctant decision and told herself she was doing it for Nadim and for no other reason. 'Fine,' she said, as blasé as she could, as if it was costing her nothing. 'I'll go to Paris.'

His dark eyes bored into hers so intensely that she started to get hot and tingly. She wanted to ask him to stop looking at her like that, but that would only give away the fact that he had an effect on her. *As if he wouldn't know that already from the wanton way she'd reacted to him in the shower.* Her lower belly felt hot.

He smiled, and her world tilted crazily. 'Good. You can stay with me.'

Jamilah faltered as she turned to leave. She looked back at him. 'But…surely you'll stay in your apartment? I can stay in a hotel.'

Salman shook his head. 'I sold that apartment years ago. I've been living in a suite at the Ritz. I have a spare room. You can stay there.'

Panic setting in, Jamilah blustered, 'I can look after my own accommodation.'

Salman waved her suggestion away. 'Don't be silly.

The meetings are taking place at the Ritz conference centre so it's the most practical solution.'

Jamilah stepped out of the plane and breathed the cool November Paris air in deep. She felt stifled, having been cooped up on a small private jet with Salman for a few hours, even though he'd kept himself to himself— surprising Jamilah by immersing himself in documents. She'd seen the headed paper and known they had to do with the meetings and that had surprised her even more. She'd fully expected him to toy with her merci- lessly during the flight, but she might as well have been invisible.

Much to her chagrin that hadn't made her feel re- lieved or...*good*.

She felt Salman nudge her back. 'Are you going to stand there all day?'

Quickly she hurried down the steps and into the wait- ing chauffeur-driven car. She heard Salman greet the driver by name, and had to assume the man was his personal driver. Within minutes they were joining the hectic stream of traffic, headed for the centre of Paris.

Emotion surged within Jamilah, despite her best at- tempts to keep it down. She hadn't been back to Paris once since that fateful time. She'd been to Nadim's sta- bles, which were just outside Paris, but not to the city. And yet here she was, *with Salman*.

Salman was acutely aware of Jamilah, resolutely facing away from him, looking out of the other window. He could see the line of her exquisite profile. Those long dark lashes. She'd tied her hair back in a chignon, and in her long dark coat she could have been any of a number of stunningly beautiful women in this city. His chest tightened. She was so much more beautiful than any of those women.

He'd had to immerse himself in work on the plane just to stop himself from giving in to a primal impulse to drag her into the sleeping cabin at the back and ravish her. And then, to his surprise, as he'd read up on the topics for the meetings he'd found his interest being stirred and ignited. For the first time in his life he'd felt something proprietorial for Merkazad rear its head. That feeling of vulnerability made his skin prickle uncomfortably.

Jamilah turned and asked huskily, 'Why did you sell your apartment?'

The unbidden answer rose up inside him. *Because I couldn't stand to live there after that day...*

Jamilah watched as something enigmatic lit Salman's eyes, and felt something in her own chest contract. But then it passed, and he looked away, shrugging. 'I grew out of it. I wasn't sure what I wanted instead, so I moved into the Ritz and I've been there ever since.'

'It must be a bit...impersonal living in a hotel?'

Salman looked back and smiled devilishly, every inch of him the supremely successful businessman in his charcoal suit and black coat. 'It suits me perfectly. And my needs.'

At the way he said *needs* Jamilah could feel colour flaring into her cheeks and looked away again. She could well imagine that it *did* serve his feckless needs. No woman being brought into the suite of a hotel would be under any illusion that their relationship wasn't as transitory as his accommodation.

Suddenly angry, Jamilah looked back, to find Salman still watching her. She reacted to that as much as to his words. 'I feel sorry for you, you know. You've cut off

all ties with your own home, you live out of a suite in
a hotel, you don't even have a relationship with your
brother—'

Her words were cut off brutally when the space between them was breached and Salman was suddenly
there. Her head was in his hands, so close to his that
she could breathe him in. She felt his powerful thighs
right against hers. Her breath came short and jerkily.
Her heart hammered.

Blisteringly he said, 'I don't need anyone's pity,
Jamilah, and I certainly don't need yours. I've made
my choices along the way, and if I had to choose again
I wouldn't do anything differently.'

At that pain lanced her so acutely that Jamilah
gasped—but it all got eclipsed when Salman's mouth
covered hers and she was thrown into the fire. Full of
emotion—anger mixed up with an awful treacherous
yearning and, unbelievably, a helpless and inexplicable
tenderness—Jamilah gripped the lapels of Salman's
coat and held him to her, matching his kiss passion for
passion. The fire was stoked higher and higher.

With a guttural groan that resonated within her, he
put his arms around her back and arched her up and into
him, so that her breasts were crushed against his hard
chest. They ached for his touch. Mouths fused again.
Jamilah's hands delved into Salman's silky hair, moulding his skull, holding him to her. In that moment she
would have gladly given everything up just for this.
This hot insanity and distraction from the pain. The
ever-present pain. Caused by this man.

That thought sliced through the frantic desire and
the pulse beating through her blood. She pulled back in
the same moment that Salman did. She was practically
supine on the back seat of the car, Salman crushing her

to the seat. She could feel the hard ridge of his erection against her thigh and her lower body throbbed painfully. She felt dishevelled, undone, and utterly exposed.

Salman lifted his head. The dark colour slashing his cheekbones and his heavy breathing sent only a sliver of comfort through Jamilah. She couldn't speak. It was only then that she noticed the privacy partition had gone up, and mortification drenched her to think of the driver witnessing this.

Salman's voice grated across her exposed nerves. 'Like I said…I don't want your pity. But I do want you. And you want me, too, Jamilah. Nothing's changed. We want each other as much as if it were that first time all over again.'

She opened her mouth to deny it, ridiculously, and Salman ruthlessly cut her off.

'*Don't* even think of saying it. You're not a liar, Jamilah. One of the things I've always admired about you is your honesty.'

She shut her mouth, and with an effort slithered out from under him, pressing her legs together and pulling her coat around her. She could feel her hair falling out of its chignon, and with shaky hands attempted to repair the damage. Her mouth felt swollen; her cheeks burned. It was futile to deny it any longer. 'I may want you, Salman, but that doesn't mean I'll go there. You washed your hands of me once already, remember?'

Salman was back on the other side of the car, his long legs spread out. His voice was tight. 'I never intended to hurt you, Jamilah. I should never have seduced you.'

Utter shock had Jamilah turning to face Salman's rigid profile. Only a deep self-preserving instinct had her saying faintly, 'I've already told you that you didn't hurt me, Salman.' *Liar.* 'What exactly are you saying?'

He flashed her a look, and she saw something indefinable in his eyes. 'I wasn't ready to let you go. I still wanted you. I've always wanted you. But I had to let you go...' his mouth twisted '...when you said you were in love with me.'

As she watched he seemed to compose himself, and that smooth mask of urbanity came back. It was as if she'd just imagined his slightly tortured look. He turned to face her more fully and said, 'But now that time has passed, and seeing as you've assured me that you're unscathed are you *sure* you want to persist in denying that this attraction is still there? After all, what do either of us have to lose now? We're both adults, experienced...'

Shock was rushing through Jamilah. She was trying to make sense of his words and at the same time make sure he couldn't see the turmoil she felt. He was saying that he'd let her go just because she'd been in love with him? That he hadn't *wanted* to let her go? It put such a new spin on what had happened that she wanted to go to a quiet place and assimilate the information... But even as she wanted that, she was aware that really it didn't change much. He'd still cast her out because he hadn't welcomed her ardent affections...

He was waiting for her response—so impassive, so implacable. Panic beat at her breast, and Jamilah cast him as cool a look as she could muster. 'I'm not interested in pursuing this line of conversation, no matter how *adult* we might be. Out of the myriad women you've no doubt entertained in your suite, I'm sure one will be available to meet your needs. Because I am not.'

Jamilah avoided Salman's eye as they drew closer to the iconic Paris hotel, feeling acutely vulnerable. As much as she might think she'd had the last word, she felt uncomfortably as if Salman had taken no heed at all and was merely biding his time to pounce.

As the car pulled in to a halt at the kerb outside the entrance of the hotel she could see doormen rush to the doors. Salman took her hand in a merciless grip and said softly, 'There's a lot to be said for slaking this desire between us, Jamilah. Here in Paris. Be done with it for good. I won't be calling up any other women because that's not what I need.' His jaw clenched as if in anger for a second. 'What I need is you…and it's the same for you. I'll be here when you're ready to admit it to yourself—because your body has already spoken.'

And then her door was being opened and she had to get out. She ripped her hand free from Salman's, saying caustically as she did so, 'Dream on, Salman.'

A short while later Salman was looking at the ornately decorated door which had just been shut in his face. A key turned in the lock at that moment as a perfunctory accompaniment, and he smiled grimly before turning and walking into the main part of the huge suite. It consisted of two bedrooms, with their own sitting rooms and *en suite* bathrooms, a formal dining room and salon, and a state-of-the-art office complete with every kind of technology for the modern businessman.

Sexual frustration pounded through his body. He'd never felt it this badly before. He was used to having his needs met, and for the first time had to face the prospect that he might just be facing his match. Determination fired his blood. He'd seen through the icy veneer that Jamilah had projected all the way up to the suite. He'd seen the pulse beating hectically under the delicate skin of her neck. She'd admitted she wanted him. He was going to woo her as he'd never had to woo a woman in his life.

With that thought in mind, and quashing the prickling of his conscience because once again he was ignoring her vulnerability, he felt the burning desire finally abate to a more manageable level, and strode into the office to take care of some work.

The following morning Jamilah felt tired and gritty-eyed after a disturbed night. She'd tossed and turned for hours in the huge luxurious bed, and had finally had to resort to *another* cold shower in the early hours of the morning. The key she had turned to lock the door on Salman the previous night might as well have been made of air; he'd still managed to infiltrate her every sleepless thought.

Now she felt more weary and exhausted than anything else as she emerged into the opulent salon. She was dressed in a dark grey pencil skirt and matching jacket, white shirt, buttoned all the way up, and black high heels. Hair pulled back into a sleek ponytail.

But nothing could have prepared her for seeing Salman standing at the main window, decked from head to toe in traditional Merkazadi robes of cream and gold, complete with turbaned headdress. He was all at once devastating and intimidating. Her heart flip-flopped ominously.

He turned and quirked a brow, reading her look instantly. 'What? I can play the part when I want to, Jamilah.'

Jamilah struggled to find her composure. She couldn't believe that seeing Salman dressed like this for the first time in years was having such an effect on her, but it was. It was transporting her right back in time to when they'd been so much younger, and he and Nadim had looked like two men old before their time at their parents' funerals. A deep melancholy assailed her and she valiantly fought down the emotion, terrified he'd see something of it.

She hitched up her chin and said, 'It's amazing how regal a robe can make one look.'

'When one is not regal at all?' He put a hand to his chest, and a mocking smile curled his lip on one side. 'You wound me, Jamilah, with your condemnation. I'm not likely ever to redeem myself in your eyes, am I?'

'I'm not here to redeem you, Salman.'

Her words struck him somewhere vulnerable and deep. Salman had to school his expression and walk over to her. 'I'm not looking for redemption or absolution from anyone.' He was unaware of the bleakness that flashed through his eyes. 'I'm looking for something else much more…earthy and immediate.'

Jamilah took a step back, unable to stand so close to him, and said briskly, 'I'm going to have breakfast downstairs. I'll see you at the first of the meetings.'

She turned and all but fled, and heard from behind her, 'Run all you want, Jamilah. It'll make the final capitulation so much sweeter.'

The main door slammed behind her on the way out, and it was a hollow and empty sound.

After a morning of intense meetings, where Jamilah stayed largely in the background as she was really only there to discuss the stables, she was reeling slightly at seeing how Salman had been so authoritative and informed. And it would appear he'd taken others by surprise, too—people who had perhaps expected him to live up to his feckless playboy reputation.

She couldn't in all honesty say that Nadim would have contributed anything more, and in fact Salman had put forward some audacious suggestions that she knew for a fact the more inherently cautious Nadim would never have sanctioned.

Now everyone was breaking for lunch, and she was trying to make a discreet escape, fully intending to find a coffee shop nearby despite the fact that lunch was being provided.

Jamilah stifled a gasp when she felt her hand being taken in a much larger one which had familiar tingles racing her up arm and into her belly. *Salman.*

He was already tugging her along in his wake, and Jamilah whispered at him, mindful of the people around them. 'I'm going out for lunch. *Alone.*'

He cast a quick glance back, and Jamilah saw the dark intent in his eyes. '*We're* going for lunch.'

'But you have to eat with the other delegates.' Desperation mounted.

Salman faced forward again, pulling her along remorselessly. 'You should know by now that I generally do not take well to orders.'

Knowing that he would not budge, nor release her, Jamilah followed with a mutinous look on her face which turned to burning embarrassment as they passed people she knew. One of them was the aide to the Sultan of Al-Omar she had abandoned at that party a year ago. She smiled weakly at him as she passed.

She could see that they were approaching the gardens at the back of the hotel. A staff member bowed deferentially to Salman as he opened a door, and then they were out in the unusually mild November air. It was a beautiful clear day that held a last lingering hint of the summer just gone.

Salman led her down a path through immaculately manicured lawns until she saw a beautifully ornate gazebo, with a table set for two, with full silver service place settings. Her stomach rumbled and she blushed.

Inside the gazebo a waiter bowed and seated them both. Totally bemused, Jamilah let him spread a snowy-white napkin across her lap, and listened while he explained about the specials on offer.

In shock, Jamilah made her choice for lunch, barely aware of what she was doing. She heard Salman say, 'I'll have the same.'

The waiter poured vintage champagne for her and sparkling water for Salman before taking his leave. A bird called nearby. The faint sound of the rumble of traffic came through the dense foliage of the bushes that climbed huge walls nearby. The gazebo was covered in trailing sweet-smelling flowers, and it was utterly secluded and idyllic.

Finally sanity returned, and Jamilah put down her napkin and stood up. 'I don't know what you're up to, Salman, but as I told you on the way here yesterday, you really should be consulting your Rolodex of contacts for this kind of thing. It's wasted on me, and I'd hate to think of you running up your tab needlessly.'

Salman affected a look of mild boredom though he felt anything but. Panic had clutched his gut when Jamilah had stood up. He knew he had to get this right or she would keep running. 'This is just lunch. I thought it might be nice to take it outside…' He waved a hand. 'I had no idea that they would put on this spectacle.'

Jamilah hesitated. There was indeed an outdoor area for dining—perhaps Salman had expected it to be there? Insecurity pierced her. Perhaps she was crediting Salman with too much ingenuity. He'd never shown any inclination for grand showy gestures when she'd been with him before…

She looked at him suspiciously. 'You really expected this to be in the other place?'

He nodded, an artful look of innocence on his face. Still thoroughly suspicious, Jamilah nevertheless found herself sitting back down, clutching her napkin. It was lunch. Just lunch. Albeit in the most seductive surroundings she'd ever encountered. Perhaps she was overreacting a little. And if she overreacted then Salman would have her in the palm of his hand.

Now she affected a look of mild uninterest. 'Fine. We don't have long for lunch anyway.' She flicked a glance at her watch. 'We have to be back in forty-five minutes.' And she sat with legs crossed, facing away from the table, as if ready to bolt.

The waiter came back at that moment with their starters. She waited to eat, suddenly very self-conscious. It was only when Salman said, with a smile playing around his mouth, 'Well? Aren't you going to eat? You must be starving…' that Jamilah gave in. She'd barely picked at breakfast that morning and nerves had curtailed her usually healthy appetite for days now.

So now, in spite of Salman's presence, she found herself all but licking her plate clean of its white asparagus starter.

Salman was sitting back, watching her, and she felt heat climb into her cheeks which she tried to disguise by wiping her mouth with her napkin. The little champagne she'd drunk was fizzing gently along her nerve-endings, making her feel all too susceptible to this…idyll. And to Salman's devastatingly dark and gorgeous presence.

'So…you are now running the stables for Nadim? Not bad for the girl who used to muck out the stalls.'

Jamilah smiled minutely. 'I still muck out the stalls, Salman. We don't stand on ceremony at the stables.'

He inclined his head and said thoughtfully, 'I can see that you would be a good boss—tough, but fair. And clearly Nadim values your opinion enough to negotiate on his behalf.'

An infusing warmth spread through Jamilah. Ever since she'd completed her studies in veterinary science in Paris, her ambition had been to manage the world-famous Merkazad stables, and to be doing it at her relatively young age was no small feat.

She shrugged lightly and avoided Salman's intense gaze. 'You know I always loved animals, I dreamed of running the stables ever since I was tiny.'

Something hollow sounded in Salman's voice. 'I know. Which is why it was good that you went home and followed your path.'

She looked at him, but his face showed no discernible emotion. And then the waiter came with their main courses and their conversation was interrupted. She'd often told him of her dreams when they'd been younger, when he'd listen in silence as she prattled on. Now she had to recall that he'd never really shared anything personal of himself—just as he hadn't in Paris. There had just been this intangible quality between them. And it still hurt to think that he'd seen her as an encumbrance.

But was he saying now that on some level he'd been concerned that she'd sacrifice her dreams for what had essentially been a fling in Paris? Coupled with what he'd revealed in the car the day before, she had to acknowledge that his rejection of her had perhaps not been as arbitrarily cruel as she'd believed it to be.

That thought made her quiet as she ate. But finally

curiosity overcame her, and she asked Salman about his own work. He wiped at his mouth with a napkin before telling her that he'd graduated to the much more risky world of hedge fund management.

He grimaced slightly. 'I'm now a part of that most reviled breed of bankers, the scourge of the recent banking crisis, and yet…' something cynical crossed his face '…reviled as we may be, business has never been so good.' He smiled, but it was without warmth.

'You have your own company?'

He nodded and took a sip of water. 'Yes, it's called Al-Saqr Holdings.'

Jamilah's fingers plucked at her napkin. 'And you don't mind being thought of…badly?'

He shrugged, eyes glinting. 'I've developed a thick skin. If people still want me to invest their money for them, to take risks on their behalf, who am I to deny them?'

'It sounds so soulless.'

'Much like living out of a hotel and leading a disconnected existence? You should know by now, Jamilah, that my soul is lost. I told you a long time ago that I'm dark and twisted inside.'

Jamilah had the shocking realisation in that moment that he really meant what he said. Why would he think that? On some level he truly *did* believe he was lost, and her heart squeezed. She could still see the boy who had come to comfort her at her parents' grave, who had instilled within her a sense of strength she sometimes still drew on. Which was ironic, when *he* was largely the reason she needed strength.

But for those three weeks he'd been gentle and infinitely generous. He'd been as she had remembered him—affectionately indulgent to her, and tolerant of her constant chatter and exuberance. But when she'd trespassed too far she'd been subjected to his icy-cold front and dismissed like all the others—cast out to the periphery.

She couldn't and would never forget his cruelty to her, but it was already becoming a more ambiguous, multi-faceted thing. Why would he feel like that about himself? What had happened to him to make him believe that? She knew if she kept on this path it would be a very dangerous one. She shouldn't be curious. She shouldn't care.

Abruptly she put down her napkin and stood up, making a hasty excuse, hating herself for it. 'I need to get some papers from the suite for my own meeting this afternoon.'

With smooth grace Jamilah saw Salman make a discreet gesture to someone behind them, and he stood up, too, indicating for her to precede him out of the gazebo. She was surprised he wasn't pushing for them to stay for coffee and dessert. She walked out a little unsteadily. And then he took her arm to lead her back into the hotel through the gorgeous private gardens.

As they neared the doors, where staff waited, she cursed her gullibility. She stopped and turned to him, looked up. 'You knew very well what you were asking for when you requested a table outside, didn't you?'

Eyes as black as sin turned her insides molten. He smiled wickedly. 'It was a mere manipulation of the truth to get you to stay.'

Jamilah fought the lazy tendrils of desire unfurling inside her. 'I don't want you to seduce me, Salman. I won't be seduced.'

'It's too late, Jamilah. We're here now…for a reason.'

His mouth firmed, 'I don't believe in fate, but I believe in *this*.'

He pulled her into him and his mouth was on hers before she could even squeak in protest. One hand went to his chest, to push him away, but his steely strength called to her, making her legs weak. She emitted a groan of pure self-disgust mixed with the inevitable rise of wanton desire. Their mouths clung, tongues touching and tasting. It grew more heated, and Jamilah found that her arms and hands had climbed up to Salman's neck and she was straining on tiptoe to get even closer.

She pulled back, her heart racing, disgusted to find herself in this position—*again*.

He held her fast against his body, where she could feel the heat and strength of his burgeoning arousal. 'Tell me again you won't be seduced...' It wasn't even a question.

Jamilah wanted to deny him, but the way she kept falling into his arms and responding so forcibly mocked her. Her heart fell at the unmistakable light of triumph in his eyes.

'The problem is that we are dealing with a force greater than ourselves, and the fact that our desire never got a chance to burn itself out,' he said.

Jamilah finally managed to pull away. 'Unlike you, I have a healthy respect for things that aren't good for me. I can resist this, and I *will*. Find someone else, Salman, *please*.' And she hoped to God that he would listen to her plea.

CHAPTER FIVE

JAMILAH had only gone back downstairs when she was due to have her own meeting with the envoy from Dubai. To her abject relief she hadn't seen Salman again, but she steeled herself now for the evening ahead, when they were due to go to a black tie function.

When she heard Salman moving around in the main salon she took a deep and shaky breath in. She regarded herself in her bedroom mirror. Make-up covered most of the ravages of the last sleepless night, and the aftermath of that lunch and the kiss. There was an awful feeling of inevitability burning low in her belly, and she couldn't ignore it much as she wanted to.

Her dress was strapless silk and floor-length, mid-night-blue in colour—almost black. It managed to be effortlessly chic even while the low back presented a much more daring view.

Her mother had been a famous fashion model—one of the first Arabic women to break into the international scene—which was how she'd met Jamilah's father in Paris. Before Jamilah's parents had died so tragically her mother had already instilled within her a love and appreciation for classic elegant clothes and jewellery. Jamilah didn't buy much, but when she did it was always quality pieces.

She'd twisted her hair up, and now added a pair of her mother's sapphire earrings to match the simple necklace that adorned her neck. With another shaky breath she picked up her short *faux* fur coat and evening bag and left her room.

Her hands clenched tight around her bag when she saw Salman, standing and flicking idly through a magazine on the table. He looked up, and for a moment Jamilah felt as if she was drowning. She'd seen Salman in a tuxedo before, but something about seeing him now, *tonight,* seemed to hit her right between the eyes. He was simply the most stupendously handsome man she'd ever seen.

Salman looked at Jamilah. She was a vision in dark silk which showed off every elegant curve of her body. Her breasts were soft pale swells above the bodice, and a gem hung with tantalising provocation just above the vee in her cleavage. Her eyes glittered a dazzling blue, and Salman knew that if they didn't get out of there right now he'd take her to his bed and she would hate him for ever. And then he had to concede bitterly that he'd already taken care of that when he'd rejected her so cruelly six years before.

Curtly, Salman said, dropping the magazine, 'We should get going, or we'll be late for the opening speech.'

Jamilah nearly reeled back on her heels. She felt as if she'd just hurtled through a time continuum, been burnt by the sun and then thrown out the other side. Had she just imagined that incendiary moment?

Standing in the lift moments later as they descended, she felt very shaky and vulnerable. Salman was stony-faced and taciturn, and it gave her a sickening sense of *déjà-vu* to when he'd changed so utterly on that fateful day six years before. She welcomed it, and hardened the tender inner part of herself that had felt an awful weakening as the day had progressed, as if on some level his relentless pursuit was starting to dissolve her own resolve to resist. She could resist. She had to resist.

Outside the hotel, in the cool night air, he helped her to put on her coat. Visibly flinching when his hand brushed the bare skin of her shoulder.

Jamilah tugged her coat from his hands and said curtly, 'It's fine. I've got it. I'm sorry you had to touch me.'

His car was just drawing up, and he turned her to face him with his hands on her shoulders. Jamilah hated that she was feeling so raw. But the stark hunger etched onto his face sent tremors of awareness through her. Along with confusion.

'You think that I don't *want* to touch you?'

Jamilah couldn't speak. In her peripheral vision she could see the driver standing and holding the door open, but they weren't moving. Salman spoke again in low husky tones.

'If I hadn't got you out of that suite as quickly as I had, I think it's safe to say that your dress would already be in ribbons and we'd be indulging in the most frantic and urgent coupling of our lives. All I can think about is how I want to pull you onto the back seat of that car, spread your legs around me and take you right now—because quite frankly the suite is too far away. I've never before contemplated stopping a lift to make love to a woman, but I just did. Don't you have any *idea* how much I want you?'

Jamilah's mouth opened and closed with shock. Any resolve that had recently fired through her was washed away by a rush of desire so intense that she literally ached for Salman to do exactly as he'd said. All she could see was their naked limbs entwined, dewed with sweat, hearts beating frantically as they came closer and closer to the explosive pinnacle.

Just then someone emerged from the hotel behind them, and Jamilah blinked as she saw Salman's urbane mask come back. It was the Sultan of Al-Omar, and she issued a garbled greeting to the tall, handsome ruler. She vaguely heard him ask if he could share their ride to the dinner, as he'd lent his car out for the evening to someone else.

Bodyguards belonging to the Sultan and to Salman hovered in the shadows, ready to jump into their accompanying vehicles. It served to bring Jamilah back to some kind of sanity, and a few seconds later she found herself pressed tight against Salman, who had negotiated it so that Jamilah was on his right, with Sultan Sadiq on his left. All Jamilah could feel was her thigh burning where Salman's pressed against her. Strong and powerfully muscular.

The men spoke of inanities and their meetings. Jamilah couldn't contribute a word, her head still whirling at Salman's intensity just now. How on earth was she going to cope if he directed that at her again? With an awful feeling of fatality she knew she wouldn't be able to.

A couple of hours later Jamilah's nerves were overwrought after an evening spent at Salman's side, trying to ignore the feelings running riot through her system. He'd barely touched her all evening, but she'd felt the burning intensity in his restraint.

Now they were back in their car—without the Sultan this time. He'd come up to Salman earlier, with a gorgeous statuesque brunette on his arm, and it had been obvious he had plans other than returning to the hotel. Sultan Sadiq had almost as notorious a reputation as Salman.

They glided through the moonlit streets of Paris now, with the Eiffel Tower appearing and disappearing intermittently, all lit up like a giant bauble. The tension was thick between them, and just when Jamilah was contemplating the uphill battle she faced if Salman tried to seduce her again she heard him ask the driver to slow down. She only noticed then that they were beside the Hôtel de Ville, where a fairground had been set up in the main square.

Salman looked at her. 'Do you mind if we get out for a minute?'

Jamilah shook her head with relief. She needed space and air in order to gather her defences again.

They got out, and when the cool air hit her she shivered. She felt Salman dropping his warm jacket around her shoulders. She looked up at him, heart tripping. 'I can get my coat. You'll freeze.'

He smiled his lopsided smile. 'I'll survive. It'll take more than the cold to do me in.'

He took her by the hand and reluctantly she gave in, knowing he wouldn't let her go anyway. They walked towards the tinkling music. Some couples were strolling around, like them, hand in hand, amongst groups of teenagers and even some harried-looking parents with small children, seemingly oblivious to the late hour.

Salman said then, so softly that she almost didn't hear him, 'I've always loved fairgrounds. There's something so escapist and other-worldly about them.'

Jamilah's mouth dropped open, and she closed it abruptly when Salman sent her an amused glance. 'Don't look so shocked.'

'When were you ever at a fairground growing up?' They had nothing like them in Merkazad.

He was leading her towards where a merry-go-round glistened under a blaze of lights. There was a melancholic quality to his voice. 'There used to be a fairground in Merkazad, but when the rebels invaded they smashed it to pieces.'

'Oh…' No wonder she hadn't ever seen one. It would have been long gone by the time she'd been old enough to visit it. 'Why wasn't another one built?'

Salman shrugged. 'I think people were having a hard enough time just rebuilding their lives and homes.'

'Perhaps someone should build one again…'

Salman looked at her with an enigmatic expression. 'Maybe one day someone will.'

The intensity of his gaze on hers made her look away and say a little breathlessly, 'You don't mind *these* horses…?'

He followed her gaze to the brightly coloured horses that went up and down and round and round. 'No,' he said tightly, 'I don't mind these horses.' He looked back at her. 'I don't mind any horses in general, Jamilah. I just choose not to go near them. I leave that up to people like you and Nadim.'

His tone brooked no further conversation, and she caught a glimpse of something suspiciously like fear in his eyes. That slightly ashen tinge again coloured his skin. She'd been around horses and people long enough to spot someone who had a pathological fear a mile away, and for the first time she guessed that Salman's antipathy to horses went far deeper than fear. It reminded her of a phobic reaction. Her curiosity was welling up again, and with it a sense of danger.

She took her hand out of his and stepped up to the

beautiful antique-looking carousel, holding her dress in one hand. She handed some money over to the man operating the controls, and when it had stopped she jumped up to sit side-saddle on one of the horses. With a burgeoning feeling of lightness in her chest she stuck her tongue out cheekily at Salman, and just as it was about to start off again he threw some money at the man and stepped up beside her, standing close enough that she could feel his hard chest against her thigh.

'Hey!' she said, breathless all over again. 'That's cheating. You're meant to sit on your own horse.'

He locked his hands around her waist and Jamilah had to hang onto his shoulders for dear life as the horse started to go up and down. They were moving. It was causing a delicious friction between his chest and her leg. He reached up and pulled her head down to his. She was powerless to resist. Their mouths met, the up and down motion of the horse forcing them close together and then apart in an intoxicating dance.

The music faded, and everything dissolved into the heat of the kiss and Salman's arms around her, holding her like an anchor. Neither one of them heard the crude wolf-whistle from a passing crowd of teens. They didn't come up for air until the man asked brusquely if they were prepared to pay for another go.

Cheeks scarlet with embarrassment, Jamilah slithered off the horse, legs wobbly, and was grateful for Salman's steadying hand on hers as he led her away. Her heart was pounding and her skin prickled with anticipation. She had no doubt that right at this moment Salman intended taking her back to the hotel and making love to her.

Maybe he was right? Maybe they *should* indulge in this madness in Paris and be purged of this crazy desire and obsession? Perhaps that was what it would take to get him out of her system for good?

Just then Salman got distracted by something. She heard the rat-tat-tat of rapid tinny gunfire coming from a shooting range, and saw where a small boy of about eight was in floods of tears because he'd obviously missed his target. His mother was trying to console him, telling him she had no more money, pleading with the owner of the stall of give him something, but the owner was sour-faced.

Before Jamilah knew what was happening Salman was striding over to the stall, dragging her along in his wake. When they reached it, he let Jamilah's hand go and bent down to talk to the little boy in perfect French. Jamilah smiled awkwardly at the beleaguered-looking mother, and wondered what Salman was up to.

After a few minutes of consulting with the now sniffling boy, who had pointed out the prize he wanted, Salman handed some money to the owner. Then he lifted up the boy and rested his feet on a rung of the fence around the stall. He helped him to aim—showing him how to balance the rifle on his shoulder, explaining how to keep a steady hand. With his arms around him, Salman encouraged the boy to take the shot. To his ecstatic surprise and the owner's evident disgruntlement he hit it first time. A perfect hit, right in the bullseye—and it was the hardest target to hit, as it was clearly the most coveted prize.

Amidst much effusive thanks, Salman finally took a bemused Jamilah's hand again, and with a wave they walked off, leaving the now chirpy boy with his grateful mum. But as they approached the car, she could sense his mood change as clearly as if a bell had gone off.

When they were in the car, Jamilah turned on a tensely silent Salman.

'Where did you learn to shoot like that?'

Salman didn't turn to face her, and just said quietly, almost as if to himself, 'I shouldn't have done that. I shouldn't have encouraged him to take the shot. It was good that he missed. Better that he be disappointed and not want to do it again than…' He trailed off.

Jamilah asked, 'Than what? Salman?'

Suddenly a chasm existed between them when minutes ago it had been all heat and urgent desire. Salman had withdrawn to somewhere impenetrable. He looked at her, but his eyes were opaque, unreadable. 'Than nothing. It doesn't matter.'

It did matter, though. She knew it with a grim certainty when she thought back to that little scene, and when she recalled the automatic way Salman had handled even a toy gun with such unerring dexterity. Like a true marksman.

Jamilah said now, 'He didn't take that shot. You did. You just made him think that he took it. It's no big deal. It's just a game.'

Salman smiled, but it was grim. 'It's never just a game.'

'How do you know this? And you didn't answer me— where did you learn to shoot?'

For such a long time he said nothing, and she almost thought he was going to ignore her, but then he said, in a scarily emotionless voice, 'It was just luck…pure fluke.'

He turned back to look out of his window, and Jamilah felt as if she'd been dismissed. The rest of the drive to the hotel was made in a silence which had thickened so much that by the time they got up to the suite Jamilah felt too intimidated to speak.

Salman just looked at her, and for a second she saw such a wealth of pain that she instinctively stepped forward with a hand outstretched. 'Salman, what is it?'

And then the enigmatic look was gone, and a stony-faced Salman said a curt, 'Nothing. Go to bed, Jamilah.'

He turned on his heel and walked into his own rooms. Thoroughly confused, Jamilah stared after him for a long moment. And then, galvanised by something she couldn't even understand, she strode forward and opened Salman's bedroom door without knocking. He was standing in the dark, looking out of the window, hands in his pockets.

He didn't turn around, just said, 'I thought I told you to go to bed.'

'You're not my father, Salman. I'll go to bed when I feel like it.'

She walked over to where he stood and looked up. When he didn't turn around exasperation made her take his arm to turn him. He looked down at her, face expressionless in the moonlight.

'What's going on, Salman? One minute you're kissing me, and the next you're treating me as if I've got leprosy.'

Salman smiled mockingly and Jamilah wanted to slap that look off his face. 'Are you saying you're ready to fall into bed with me?'

He cast a look at his watch and gave a low whistle. 'Not bad. It only took twenty-four hours. I was convinced it would take at least two days. Was it my concern for the boy's distress that melted your soft-hearted resistance, or was it the impressive way I wielded the gun?'

Jamilah's hand came up then, and she did slap him. Hard enough to make his head turn. Her hand tingled and burned. Shakily she said, 'You deserved that—and not for what you just said, but for what you did to me six years ago.'

She turned and walked to the door, and Salman said softly from behind her, 'Make no mistake, Jamilah, I do want you. But if we sleep together I won't and can't offer you anything more than I offered last time.' Bitterness rang in his voice. 'At least you can't say that I'm not warning you up-front.'

Jamilah turned back. 'Go to hell, Salman.'

As she turned again and walked away she heard him say quietly, 'I've already been there for a long time.'

Something stopped her in her tracks at that. She turned again, despite all the screaming voices and warning bells going off in her head. 'What's that supposed to mean?'

CHAPTER SIX

SALMAN heard Jamilah's words, and his whole body contracted as if from a physical blow. Damn the woman, why wouldn't she just leave? A voice mocked him. *Like the way you forced her to leave six years ago?*

A wave of weariness nearly knocked Salman sideways then. He'd been so rigid, so controlled, so angry for so long. And this woman was taking a sledgehammer to all of that and smashing it aside without even knowing what she was doing.

Grimly he turned to face her, his face still stinging from her slap. He welcomed it.

When Jamilah saw the lurid print of her hand on Salman's cheek in the shadows she felt huge remorse. She came forward on stiff legs, and in a rush made a stilted apology for hitting him. She'd never hit another human being in her life, and was genuinely mortified at her behaviour.

But he just said grimly, 'I'm not sorry you hit me. I deserved it. And I probably deserve more.'

Jamilah shook her head. 'I don't get it, Salman. It's almost as if you want to be punished.'

He cracked a tight smile. 'Don't I?'

Jamilah was silent. She suspected he wasn't referring to his behaviour six years ago with her—or he was, but it was only a small part of a much bigger thing. 'What really happened with that boy tonight? Why did it affect you like that?'

Salman looked at her for a long moment, his dark gaze blistering her for her question, but as he did so she felt more and more defiant. She wasn't going to back down.

And then he said tightly, 'I don't think you really want to know why.'

Sudden anger flared that he should shut her out like this. She sensed that this was at the very core of who he was. 'Don't patronise me, Salman. I'm sure there's nothing you could tell me that would unduly shock me.'

That bleakness flashed across his face again before it was masked. He smiled grimly. 'Nevertheless, it's not something I want to discuss right now.'

Without even really thinking about what she was saying Jamilah asked, 'When *will* it be the right time, Salman?'

His mouth tightened. 'For you? Never. I would never do that to you.'

'You already did, Salman.'

She knew they were talking about two different things now, and yet it was all inextricably bound up together—Salman's dark secrets and the way he'd treated her, the way he still didn't trust her enough to reveal himself. And never would.

A sense of futility made her turn as if to go, but to her shock and surprise Salman grabbed her wrist and said tightly, 'Are you sure you really want to know, Jamilah?'

She faced him slowly and could see the intense glitter of his eyes, the way a muscle pulsed in his jaw. The moment was huge, and she knew that much of their history and this present madness was bound up in it.

Slowly, as if she might scare him off, she nodded her head. 'Yes, I want to know, Salman.'

Salman looked into Jamilah's huge blue eyes. He had the most bizarre sensation of drowning while at the same time clinging onto a life-raft. He couldn't believe he'd stopped her from leaving—couldn't believe he'd just said what he had. Did he really think he was about to divulge to her what no one else knew? His deepest, darkest shame? And yet in that instant he knew an overwhelming need to unburden himself here, with *her*. It could never have been with anyone else. He saw that now, as clear as day.

That little boy had had a more profound effect on him than he'd expected. He'd acted completely on instinct to go and comfort him, and when he'd seen what he could do to make him feel better he'd done it. It had only been afterwards, walking away, when the full impact of taking that shot had hit him.

His past had rushed upwards to slap him in the face far harder than Jamilah ever could. For a few moments in that fairground with Jamilah he'd been seduced by her all over again. Seduced into a lighter way of being. Seduced into thinking that he *didn't* carry around an awful legacy and a dark secret which pervaded his being like a poison.

The bravery he'd witnessed from others mocked him now—was he afraid to do this? For the first time he knew he wasn't. What he *was* afraid of, right here and now, was how Jamilah would react to what he was about to tell her…for if anything could drive her away for good *this* could. Perhaps this was the sum total of his actions—to be brought to his knees by her only to watch her walk away for good.

Jamilah watched as Salman clearly struggled with something, but then his face became expressionless. The light spilling in from the sitting room illuminated its stark lines and he'd never looked so bleak. He dropped her wrist, and it tingled where he had held it. He walked over to a chair in the corner and sat down heavily, and Jamilah, not taking her eyes off him, perched on the end of the bed. Her throat had gone dry.

His head was downbent, and then he lifted it, that black gaze spearing her. 'What I said to you that day in Paris…about how there had never been anything between us, about you following me around like a puppy dog…it was a lie.'

For a second a buzzing sounded in Jamilah's ears. She thought she might faint. As much as she wanted to deny that she remembered his cruel words, she said instead, 'Why? Why did you say it?' Relief was a giddy surge through her body.

'I said it because you'd told me you loved me, and I knew that if I didn't make you hate me you might not stay away. You might hope you could change me.'

He smiled then, and it was grim. 'But then, as you've said yourself, what you felt was merely a crush, so perhaps I needn't have been so cruel.'

Jamilah would have laughed if she'd had the where-withal at this understatement of the year. She hoped the pain she felt wasn't evident in her voice. 'You wanted me gone that badly?'

'Yes. Because I couldn't take the responsibility of your love. Because I couldn't return it. Because I *can't*.' He was warning her even now not to expect too much.

Suddenly Jamilah wanted them off this topic. 'Tell me what you're going to tell me, Salman.'

As bleak as she'd ever seen him, he said now, his eyes intent on her, 'I know that I have to tell you. I owe you that much now.'

Jamilah nodded, and wondered why on earth she felt an awful foreboding.

Salman looked down at his hands for a long moment, and then began to speak in an emotionless voice—as if to try and distance himself from what he said. 'The week after my eighth birthday Merkazad was invaded. We'd had no warning. We had no reason to believe that we were in any danger. But unbeknownst to us the Sultan of Al-Omar had long wanted to reclaim Merkazad as part of his country. He resented our independence.'

Jamilah knew all this—and about how the current Sultan's father had been the one to launch an invasion with his most ruthless men. She nodded, even though Salman wasn't looking at her.

'We were sent to the dungeons while they ransacked and looted all around the castle. It took time for the rest of their men to arrive, thanks to our belated Bedouin defence kicking in, which held them off, but we were effectively trapped in the castle with the soldiers and any kind of rules of war went out of the window. These were men hardened by their experiences—the elite soldiers of the army.'

He looked up and smiled at Jamilah, but it was so cold that she shivered.

'They got bored. And so they wanted to amuse themselves. They decided to take me on as a pet project of sorts. To see how long it would take to turn a pampered son of the Sheikh into something else...something more malleable.'

A slow trickling of horror started to snake through Jamilah. She went very still.

'Every day they would come…and take me out of the gaol they'd made out of our old dungeon. At first I bragged to Nadim. I told him that it was because they favoured me. He'd always been the strong one, the one everyone looked up to, and now *I* was the one being singled out. I couldn't understand my mother and father's terror, and if they spoke up too much they were beaten. For the first few days they let me be the cocky little spoilt boy I was—precocious and undoubtedly annoying. We played games…football. They fed me well, made sure I had enough to drink.'

Salman's mouth thinned, his jaw clenched.

'And then it started. The breaking down. The food and drinks were denied me. They started beating me with fists and feet, belts and whips, for the smallest thing. I was bewildered at first. I'd thought they'd been my friends and suddenly they weren't. When I was brought back to the gaol in the evenings I wasn't so cocky. I was confused. How could I explain to Nadim what was going on? I couldn't understand it myself. And yet I couldn't ask for his help. I was too proud, even then. But he suspected what they were doing, and he begged them to take him instead. They ignored him and took me. And they told me that if I didn't go with them every day they would kill Nadim and my parents.'

Jamilah already had a lump in her throat. She wanted to ask Salman to stop, but knew she couldn't. If there was ever to be any hope of closure between them then she had to endure this.

Salman shook his head as if to dislodge a memory. 'The days morphed into one long day… There's a lot I don't remember, but eventually the beatings stopped. By then I was no longer confident, cocky or spoilt. They'd broken me. I had become their tea boy—their servant. They made me polish their boots, make them their lunch.' He took a deep breath. 'But then they got bored again, and decided to train me to be just like them—ruthless soldiers. So they gave me a gun and took me down to the stables for some target practice.'

'Salman...' Jamilah let out a low, horrified breath, shaking her head in denial of what was to come.

He smiled grimly. 'After it was over—when we were free—the thing that upset my father the most was the fact that they'd shot all the horses. Except they hadn't...it was *me*. I was forced to use the horses as target practice, and I got very good very quickly once they told me I had only one shot per horse. If I didn't succeed first time they would let the horse die in agony.'

Jamilah closed her eyes. *That* was why he knew how to use a gun. And that was why he never went near horses or the stables. She opened her eyes. She felt as if a cold wind was blowing over her soul. She was numb, and knew it was the protection of shock. 'Abdul defended you one day at the stables...I couldn't understand why...'

A muscle clenched in his jaw. 'That first day Abdul tried to stop them, and they offered me a choice. Either start killing the horses or kill *him*. It wasn't a choice. Worse than anything, though, was that they made me into one of *them*. I had to start thinking like them just to survive. I had to become wily. The day the Bedouin came and rescued us they found me up on the roof of the castle with a gun. I'd somehow got away from the rebels and was going to try and shoot them...' His mouth twisted. 'I was wild, feral... I was about to kill another

human being because they had desensitised me so much
that I believed it not only possible but acceptable.'

She felt sick. 'How can you even bear to go to
Al-Omar after that?'

Salman shook his head. 'Sultan Sadiq is not his father.
He and Nadim made a peace agreement years ago. And
he personally oversaw the arrest and imprisonment of
all the rebel elements of his father's army.'

Without even thinking about what she was doing
Jamilah kicked off her shoes and padded barefoot over
to where Salman sat. She knelt at his feet, took one of
his hands in hers, and looked up at him, an unbelievable
ache in her chest. 'I had no idea that such terror was
visited upon you. Why does no one know this?' She
felt the tension in his frame.

'Because I blamed myself for a long time. I believed
that I'd been responsible on some level—that I'd invited their attention. How could I tell my father what I'd
done? He'd never forgive me...or at least that was what I
thought. I had nightmares for years of being pursued by
a herd of wild avenging horses until I was so exhausted
that I would fall and they would trample me to death.'

Jamilah shook her head, gripping his hand. 'It wasn't
your fault.'

Salman quirked a weary smile. 'It's one thing to
know that on an intellectual level, and another entirely
to believe it with all your being.'

Abruptly he stood up, forcing her to stand, too. He
took his hand from hers and tipped his head back, his
features suddenly stern. 'So now you know. I hope the
lurid tale was worth the wait...'

Jamilah shook her head. 'Salman, don't...'

Salman was reacting to how exposed and naked he
felt in that moment—alternately drawn to and wanting

to escape from Jamilah's huge eyes, which swirled with emotions he couldn't bear to acknowledge. 'Salman, don't *what?* I told you I was twisted and dark inside, and now you know why. Nothing else has changed, Jamilah. I still want you.' His mouth thinned. 'But I won't be surprised if you find your desire suddenly diminished. Not many people relish a battle-scarred lover. Perhaps I *should* take your advice and go and slake my lust elsewhere.'

The stoic pride on his face, mixed with a vulnerability she'd never seen before, made her want to weep. Jamilah fought not to contradict him vociferously. How could he think that? She remained silent, stunned by his awful revelations. She was reeling, in shock and numb all over, but she finally managed to get out, 'What you've told me hasn't disgusted me at all…you were a victim, and shouldn't have had to go through that alone.'

Jamilah sensed Salman's volatility, sensed his anger that he'd revealed what he had. She knew it must have cost him, and he wouldn't welcome the fact that she'd all but bludgeoned him into it. She had to walk away now or he might see how badly she wanted to step up to him, pull his head down and comfort him. She tore her gaze from his and turned and walked away.

At the door she stopped, but didn't turn back. All she said was, 'I'm glad you told me, Salman.' And she left.

For long moments after Jamilah had left the room Salman just stood there, in shock at how easily he'd let his darkness spill out, and at Jamilah's sweetly accepting response. He'd seen pity, yes, but it hadn't made him feel as constricted as he might have imagined. He'd always dreaded the reaction he might get. That was why he found it so easy to listen to others tell their tales.

There was an intense battle raging within him: to take Jamilah and slake his lust, drown himself in the sanctuary that he suspected with grim certainty only she could give him, or to push her away so far and so fast that she would be protected from him. *Again.*

And yet just now she hadn't run from him in horrified terror at the images that had haunted him all his life. He'd seen the compassion in her eyes and had recoiled from it, even as he'd wanted to bury his head in her breast and beg her to never let him go. He who'd never sought comfort from anyone! Even in the darkest moments, when he'd felt he was going mad with all the nightmares and memories.

The parameters of their relationship had just shifted, and Salman wasn't sure where they stopped and started any more. All he knew was that he *wanted* her—now more than ever. Even while he felt that need he acknowledged that after tonight she would have to come to him, but the question was, would she?

Jamilah lay in bed, wide awake, her stomach roiling at the thought of what Salman had gone through. Her head was whirling with all the information. So much made sense now: that terrible darkness that was like a cloak around him, his frosty relationship with Nadim and Merkazad, his fear of horses… And yet he also seemed to be even more of an enigma. She now knew his inner demons, but she'd never felt further from knowing *him*.

Jamilah turned over onto her side and looked out onto the empty square that housed the iconic hotel. Moonlight lit up the monument in the middle, throwing it into stark relief. Despite everything Salman had told her, what was at the forefront of her mind was the

fact that he'd lied about their bond being non-existent.
That he'd said it purely to drive her away. And it had
worked—admirably.

She had to concede now that if he had been nicer
about rejecting her perhaps a doubt always would have
lingered, torturing her even more? Perhaps she wouldn't
have left and got on with her life and career?

Eventually she fell into an uneasy sleep, full of dark
dreams and scary faces with no features, and when she
woke in the morning, nearly late for her first meeting,
she was relieved to see that Salman had already left the
suite.

In the cold light of day what he'd endured seemed to
be so much starker and worse. She sensed that he was
waiting for her to make the next move, and in all honesty
she didn't know if she had the strength to resist him any
more…not with this new knowledge in her head and,
worse, this desire to comfort him, heal him in some
way. She was very much afraid that his cataclysmic
confession had torn what remained of her defences to
pieces, and now she'd have nothing to hide behind. Not
even anger.

That night, after another elaborate dinner, which had
been held in their own hotel this time, Jamilah accepted
an invitation from the Sultan of Al-Omar's aide to go
for a drink to the bar. She'd always felt guilty about how
she'd run out on him at the Sultan's party the previous
year, after that tense meeting with Salman.

At least that was the justification for her agreeing
to the drink. In truth she'd been avoiding Salman all
day, still too raw to be able to deal with him and that
penetrating dark gaze now that she knew the reason for
the shadows behind it. But she'd known where he was at

every moment, and she'd seen how his eyes had flashed when he'd noticed her leaving with Ahmed just minutes before.

Earlier that evening she'd been ready before Salman, and had gone down to dinner without him. She'd congratulated herself, having managed to successfully avoid him yet again. But when he'd arrived at dinner he'd raked her whole body across the room with a look so hot she'd been surprised little fires hadn't broken out over her skin. She'd thought her dress was modest enough— vee-necked silk, with a tight waist and full skirt to the knee—but one look from Salman and she'd feared he'd melted it right off her.

'*Jamilah.*'

Jamilah flinched and looked at Ahmed, and smiled apologetically.

'I'm sorry, my mind is miles away…' She put a hand on his arm. It wasn't fair of her to be here with him when she couldn't concentrate on their conversation. 'Look, I think we should take a raincheck. I'm not great company this evening.'

Ahmed smiled ruefully, and Jamilah wished that she found the perfectly nice-looking man half as attractive as she found Salman.

'This wouldn't have anything to do with Salman al Saqr, would it?'

Jamilah coloured as Ahmed stood up and waited for her to stand, too.

He said as they walked out, 'Don't worry, it's not that obvious, but I've been in close proximity to you two before, if you remember.'

Jamilah went hotter when she recalled Ahmed finding them in the corridor, with tension crackling between them. She couldn't lie as she followed him out of the bar and to the lifts. 'He's got a little to do with it, I guess.'

In the lift Ahmed turned to her and said, somewhat stuffily, 'I know you won't want to hear this, but he *has* got a reprehensible reputation with women.'

Jamilah just managed to stifle a hysterical laugh. Poor Ahmed didn't know the half of it. But she appreciated his concern. He walked her to the door of the suite and she smiled at him, feeling sad. And then something rose up within her—a sense of desperate futility as she thought of Salman and the impossibility of their relationship. Perhaps if she just gave someone else a chance…

She moved closer to Ahmed and asked, 'Can I kiss you?'

The other man looked comically shocked, and his glasses practically steamed up as he blustered, 'Yes… of course.'

He moved forward awkwardly, and in that moment Jamilah knew it was all wrong—she shouldn't have said anything. But it was too late. His hands were around her waist, gripping too tightly, and then he was bumping her nose, aiming for her mouth before planting a fleshy wet kiss on her lips.

In a move so fast that she didn't know which way was up Jamilah heard a door open and found herself being pulled back and out of Ahmed's hands. Her relief quickly disappeared when she realised that it was Salman who now gripped her waist. She could feel his tall, taut strength behind her and her body reacted accordingly. Poor Ahmed was clearly terrified.

He backed away and said a garbled goodnight, then fled. Salman whirled Jamilah around in his arms, and all she could do was open and close her mouth ineffectually.

The difference between this man and Ahmed was comical. Her body was rejoicing as if it had just found its long-lost mate. Her hands were fists on his chest. He was still in his ceremonial robes, no tuxedo tonight, and she was very aware of his body through the insubstantial flimsiness of her silk cocktail dress.

He tugged her into the room with him, and her back thudded against the door when Salman slammed it shut. He crowded her, his hands by her head, eyes blistering down into hers. 'What the hell was that about?' He mocked her voice. *"Can I kiss you?"'*

Jamilah welcomed the surge of anger at his arrogant behaviour. It helped to distract her from dealing with the fact that facing this man made her feel so exposed and raw and *emotional*. 'It's rude to listen at doors and spy through peepholes. And who gave you the God-given right to order Ahmed off like that?'

Salman grimaced. 'I didn't say a word. He knew he wasn't wanted—just as he wasn't wanted last year. He looked like he was about to drown you in drool.'

Jamilah shuddered at the memory, even though she tried to hide it.

Salman went very still. 'I disgust you now. That's it, isn't it? Your head is full of awful images and I put them there.'

To Jamilah's surprise, Salman released her from the cage of his arms and swung away, energy blistering from him. Instinctively Jamilah reached out and took Salman's arm. 'No—*no,* Salman. Of course you don't disgust me.'

He wouldn't turn round, and said tautly, 'I felt your reaction just now. You'd prefer to be kissed by that toad than me.'

Jamilah's brain was blank for a moment, and then she

remembered her reaction to the thought of being kissed by Ahmed, the violent shudder that had run through her. She came and stood in front of Salman. He looked so proud and handsome. How could he possibly think…?

Salman still battled the jealousy that had ripped through him like corrosive acid when he'd watched Jamilah walk out of the ballroom with that man. He shook with it. And when he'd seen them kiss just now he'd gone blind with rage. He couldn't even look at Jamilah as she stood in front of him now. He'd never felt so exposed and weak in front of anyone. Not even those soldiers had reduced him to this.

Jamilah burned as she looked up and saw the intensity on Salman's face, the way he avoided her eye. Anger had turned into something much more ambiguous and explosive within her. A treacherous tenderness was rushing through her—exactly what she'd been afraid of all day. She would have to make the first move, to show him, prove to him, that she wanted him, and she could no more deny him that than stop breathing.

This was their moment of reckoning. She knew that much. A reckless exhilaration was thrumming through her blood now—and it had been from the moment he'd replaced Ahmed's hands with his own. In her head she finally capitulated to her most base desires and threw caution to the wind, saying, 'If you can't see that my reaction was for Ahmed, and not you, then you're losing your touch, Salman. You don't disgust me. Quite the opposite, in fact. So why don't you just shut up and kiss me?'

She'd shocked him as much as herself. She could feel it in the sudden tension in his body. He looked down at her and she wound her arms around his neck, for the first time feeling a little in control of the situation. She went up on tiptoe and pressed her mouth to Salman's. And then, when he didn't move, she pulled back and said, 'What's the matter, Salman? Can't you handle a woman taking the initiative?'

His hands went to her waist and burned through her clothes. 'Oh, I can handle it, all right, but I just want to know this: are you *sure* you know what you're doing?'

Jamilah shut out the cacophony of warning voices in her head and pressed even closer to Salman, exulting in the feel of his hard erection between them. 'I know exactly what I'm doing. I can take care of myself. I have been for a long time now.'

CHAPTER SEVEN

SALMAN smiled, and it was feral, and it made something deep inside Jamilah shiver with anticipation. 'I think I like you even more when you're dominant and bossy.'

Before she could make a retort Salman was walking her back until she felt herself thud against the door again. His head descended, and nothing but delicious heat and sensation concerned Jamilah any more. She held him close, fingers tangling in his hair. Their tongues duelled fiercely, as if they couldn't get enough of one another.

She'd hungered for him for too long. Desire was overflowing and all-encompassing, and she didn't have a hope of resisting—not that she could have after her provocative little speech. Jamilah had no idea where that confidence had come from, but knew she'd gone that route in a bid to feel as if she was the one in control.

But that and every other coherent thought fled when she felt Salman's hands on her back, pulling down the zip of her dress. His mouth left hers and followed the line of her jaw down to her shoulder, where she could feel him pulling down the strap of her dress. Her breath came jerkily, her hands dropped, and she sagged back against the door, her legs trembling. They'd gone from zero to a thousand in thirty seconds on the arousal scale.

Salman pulled the strap down her arm and she could feel her dress gaping open at the back. Nothing could stop it from falling down now, and exposing one bare breast. In the dim light he pulled back for a moment and looked his fill. All Jamilah could do was concentrate on not passing out with the intensity of the desire pulsing through her. She felt her breast grow heavy, and its peak tightened unbearably. She bit her lip to stop herself from begging Salman to touch her there.

She felt so wanton, and almost cried out when Salman cupped the fleshy weight and said throatily, 'So beautiful…I've dreamed of this, Jamilah. I've dreamed of *you*.'

His thumb passed back and forth over the throbbing peak, and when he bent his head and licked around it before sucking it into his mouth she did cry out, holding his head with her hands.

Desperation mounted through her as the memory of the bliss only he could evoke was awoken within her core. 'You…' she said breathily. 'I want to see you.'

Salman stopped his luxurious lavishing of attention on her breast and stood up. With sheer sensual grace and ease of confidence he tugged off his outer robe, and then the thinner under-robe. He kicked off his shoes, his eyes never leaving Jamilah's even though she couldn't help but look down and take her fill of his magnificent broad chest. He'd changed since she'd last seen him naked. He'd filled out even more and was truly *a man*. Broad-shouldered and leanly muscular.

The loose pants barely clung to his narrow hips, and his hands went there to undo the tie. Within seconds they'd fallen to the floor and he stood before her naked and proud, his erection making her eyes go wide. She'd forgotten how big he was.

He came close again, and tipped up her chin with a finger. Then he slid the other strap of her dress down the other arm until her dress fell to her waist. With a gentle tug from his hands it joined his clothes on the floor. Now all she wore were black lace panties and her high heels. Salman looked down her body. Jamilah could feel little fire trails wherever his eyes rested, and between her legs she was aching for his touch.

He reached and took the pin out of her hair, letting it fall around her shoulders, and then he said huskily, 'Are you wet for me, Jamilah?'

Jamilah groaned softly in eloquent answer as Salman trailed his index finger down and through the valley of her cleavage. She'd been wet for him since the moment she'd heard the helicopter bring him back to Merkazad.

And then she groaned even louder as Salman dropped to his knees before her and slipped one shoe off and then the other, looking up at her, black eyes glittering wickedly. 'I want to taste you.'

He pulled her panties down over her hips, down her legs and off. Then he gently pushed her legs apart before taking her right leg and hooking it over his shoulder, opening her up to him.

Jamilah was gone beyond any point of return, and had to put a fist to her mouth when she felt his breath feather through her dark curls. His tongue lashed out and laved her secret inner folds, finding where her clitoris throbbed for attention. She was a helpless captive to this sensual onslaught. She bit her hand, her body spiralling towards the most intense orgasm she'd ever had as Salman licked without mercy until everything exploded around her and went black for a second, her whole body throbbing in the aftermath.

He held her legs when she would have collapsed in a heap, their support completely gone. When she'd recovered enough to focus again, he rose up in a smooth move and lifted her into his arms. Jamilah was boneless. But being held in Salman's arms with her naked breasts against his chest was making little tremors of arousal start up all over again.

This was how it had been between them—intense and furious. Every time. Salman laid her down gently on his bed and stood up to look at her for a long moment. His intent gaze made her feel sensual and womanly. His obvious arousal made a heady pleasure wash through her in waves. But then she couldn't stand it any longer. She held out a hand. 'Salman…I want you.'

To her relief he came down on two hands over her and said gruffly, 'I want you, too. So much it hurts.'

She twined her hands around his neck and pulled him down on top of her, relishing his heavy weight and that potent hardness between her legs. She spread her legs wide and said huskily, 'Show me where it hurts and I'll kiss it better.' She wasn't unaware of the symbolism of her kissing away his hurts, of wanting to *heal* him, and emotion made her chest full.

He touched a finger to his mouth. 'Here…'

Jamilah reached up and pressed her mouth to his, her tongue darting out to lick and taste, teeth nipping gently at his lower lip.

She pulled back and Salman's eyes glittered. He pointed to his chest, 'Here, too…'

Jamilah ran her hands down the sides of his powerful torso, feeling a shudder run through him, and pressed her open mouth to his chest, moving down to find a blunt nipple and licking him there before tugging gently on the hard nub.

He shifted back and his erection slid tantalisingly along the moist folds of her sex. Jamilah's hips lifted towards him instinctively. She ached for him so badly that she moaned in despair when he moved away for a moment to don protection.

But then he was back, pressing down on top of her, kissing her hungrily. With a powerful move he thrust into her, making her gasp at the sensation. It had been so long for her that she was tight, and she shifted to accommodate Salman's length.

As Salman started to move, though, the tightness eased, and she could feel that delicious tension building and building. A light sweat broke out on her skin. She wrapped her legs around Salman's back, causing him to slide even deeper, and she felt his chest move against her breasts with his indrawn breath. With ruthless and relentless precision he brought them higher and higher, until there was nowhere else to go. For a second Jamilah felt a moment of fear at the intensity of the climax about to hit, and when it did all she could do was cling on to Salman until she felt him tense, and then the powerful contractions of her orgasm sent him over the edge, too.

For a long moment there was nothing but the sound of their ragged breathing and the pounding of their hearts. Salman eased his weight off her and she felt suddenly bereft, and hated herself for feeling like that. She remembered from before that Salman had never really indulged in post-coital tenderness, so she was shocked when he reached for her and pulled her into him, wrapping his arms around her, cradling her bottom with his thighs. She could feel him, still semi-hard, and blushed.

She lay there for a long time, listening to Salman's

breaths deepen and even out. She couldn't sleep. She was too wound up in the aftermath. She recalled her blatant provocation of Salman and winced. He might have shown her a more vulnerable side of himself than she'd ever seen, and he might have revealed that he hadn't intended to be so cruel in his rejection of her, but she knew that he would not welcome recognising that. He was too proud, had been invulnerable for too long. And he would lash out.

Wanting to be gone when he woke, dreading seeing his mocking visage at her easy capitulation, she carefully extricated herself from his arms and reached for a robe that was at the end of the bed. She pulled it on and tied it with shaking hands. She looked at Salman, lying sprawled on the bed like a marauding king or a pirate, and before he could wake walked out of the room and straight to her own, where she went into the bathroom, dropped the robe, and stepped into a hot shower.

She willed the tears not to come, hating herself for her weakness. Suddenly all her recent bravado was gone and she was the same soft-hearted naïve Jamilah, who hadn't learnt a thing about self-protection. Suddenly she heard a sound, and whirled around to see a naked Salman standing at the door of her shower. Ridiculously she covered her breasts and spluttered, 'What the——?'

He was grim. 'I'd bet money right now that you haven't slept with anyone in a long time. You were almost as tight as the first time we slept together.'

Water was getting into Jamilah's eyes, and humiliation nearly made her feel nauseous. She spluttered again. 'That is none of your business.'

'Well, if it's any consolation, I haven't been able to sleep with anyone since I kissed you at the Sultan's party last year.'

Salman stepped into the steam of water and it sluiced down his olive-skinned body. His admission took the sting out of Jamilah's humiliation. 'You haven't?'

He shook his head. 'No. Not until I saw you again have I wanted to touch anyone.'

'But…the blonde woman in the castle that morning?'

He grimaced and said curtly, 'She followed me and wouldn't get out of my room. I hadn't slept in nights, and I was too exhausted to carry her out.'

He hadn't touched her yet, and Jamilah's hands were still over her breasts. Salman reached out and took them down. His eyes turned sultry and dark, and all Jamilah's recent feelings of recrimination dissolved like ice on a hot coal. She was mesmerised by his statement and by him.

He took some soap and started to lather it up, and then his hands smoothed over every part of her body, soaping and washing. She leant back against the wall, her eyelids heavy, and could only watch as Salman became more and more visibly aroused. He turned her round and came up behind her, snaking arms around her to cup her soapy breasts in his hands, his fingers trapping her nipples until she squirmed against him, his erection sliding tantalisingly between the globes of her bottom.

She felt him reach down over her belly and lower, between her legs, to where she was hot and slippery with renewed arousal. He muttered roughly, 'I can't wait… put your hands on the wall…'

She obeyed him wordlessly, and felt him pull her back more, then spread her legs. With a keening cry of frustration she felt him guide himself between her legs, until he could surge up and into her heat.

One hand touched her, flicking her clitoris, his other

hand was on her breast, kneading and moulding the weighty flesh. Jamilah gasped for breath, struggling to retain some sanity as the water sluiced over them, heightening everything.

The climax came swiftly, rolling over them like a huge wave and throwing them high. Jamilah gasped, head flung back, as Salman pounded into her, every powerful thrust of his body sending her hurtling into another climax. With one final thrust he stilled, and she felt his release spill deep inside her. Only the faintest of alarm bells went off. She was too stunned, trembling all over in the aftermath.

Salman gently turned her around and gathered her close, settling his mouth over hers in a brief kiss. 'Are you okay?'

Jamilah could only nod. She was speechless, and just let Salman lift her out of the shower and wrap her in a huge towel. She'd been wrong. It had never been like this before. It had been amazing, yes. But this...this transcended everything that she had experienced with this man before. It was as if she'd had an extra layer of skin before, but now it was gone. And in a way it was; she was no longer an idealistic virginal innocent...

He dried her, before drying himself, and wrapped her hair in a towel. He hitched another towel around his waist and led her out to the bedroom, to sit beside her on the end of the bed.

Jamilah's brain was still numb from an excess of sensation and pleasure. Slowly reality trickled back, and Jamilah saw that Salman had his arms resting on his legs, head downbent. As if he could feel the weight of her gaze, he looked up. She saw that there was a grim set to his face.

'I didn't use protection.'

An old pain made Jamilah feel weak inside. She hadn't even noticed that they hadn't used protection. She forced out through numb lips, 'It should be fine. I'm at a safe stage of my cycle…'

She looked away, to a spot on the floor, and knew in that moment that she had to tell him what had happened. She didn't know if it was out of a desire to inflict pain because he'd made her feel so vulnerable, or out of a genuine necessity to let him know that for a brief moment he'd been a father.

She said quietly, 'Anyway, I'd know if I was pregnant after a couple of weeks.'

She could feel his look, his frown. 'What do you mean? How would you know?'

She took a shaky breath. 'Because I was pregnant before and the symptoms hit me almost immediately. But about a month after I fell pregnant I lost the baby.'

He turned her to face him, but instead of seeing the dawning of understanding all she saw was compassion. 'Is that why it's been so long since you were with anyone?'

It took a long second for her to realise that he wasn't putting two and two together. Could he really be so obtuse? Jamilah wanted to laugh and cry at the same time. And suddenly her desire to tell him the truth faded. What purpose would it serve when he clearly couldn't believe for a second that she spoke about *him?* And after everything he'd told her last night? Treacherously, she didn't want to give him something else to feel guilty about, and she hated herself for that weakness because it meant she was just as lost to him all over again.

She brushed his hand aside and said, 'Something like that… Look, I'm really quite tired. I'd like to go to sleep now. *Alone.*'

To her intense relief, after a long moment when he clearly didn't know what to do with the information she'd just given him, he said, 'Are you sure you want to be alone?'

Jamilah nodded, and with a last look Salman got up and left the room. Jamilah got into the bed with the towels still wrapped around her hair and her body. She curled up in a ball as silent tears trickled down her cheeks and she grieved for the baby who'd never had a chance.

Salman lay awake for a long time, thinking about what Jamilah had revealed. Hearing that she'd been pregnant with another man's child sent all sorts of ambiguous emotions to his gut. One in particular felt very similar to the jealousy he'd felt earlier.

He'd always vowed to himself that he wouldn't bring a child into this overpopulated world. The main reason being that he was quite simply terrified that he wouldn't be able to protect it from the terrors that were out there. From the terrors that he himself had witnessed, which he felt were indelibly marked in his blood and might possibly be passed down to a son or daughter. That was why he'd taken the drastic decision to have a vasectomy nearly ten years previously.

He'd mentioned his lapse about protection more out of a concern to keep them both safe from disease or infection. But Jamilah, understandably enough, had assumed he'd been concerned about pregnancy. He hadn't corrected her as he'd never told anyone about the vasectomy. But just thinking of it brought his mind back to how it had felt to take Jamilah like that, skin on skin, and arousal flared all over again.

He grimaced and rolled over, punching a pillow

before settling his head on it. He could see now what had added shadow and depth to Jamilah in the intervening years, and curiously Salman had to battle down an urge to find out more…to protect.

The following day Jamilah felt paranoid—as if everyone was looking at her. Could they see where it felt as if a layer of skin had been stripped off her body? Thankfully she was caught up in meetings for most of the day, so she didn't have to cope with facing Salman. Eventually she went to the bathroom to see if there *was* something on her face, and grimaced at her reflection. Despite the fact that she'd not had a good night's sleep her skin glowed, and her eyes were so bright they looked almost feverish.

Her lips seemed to be swollen, and they tingled at the memory of Salman's kisses. As if on cue she felt her breasts tighten and her nipples harden against the lace of her bra. She wanted him even now. She stifled a groan of despair.

Just then an acquaintance came out of a cubicle.

Jamilah composed herself and smiled at the woman, and washed her hands. The other woman smiled back, and was about to go, but then she turned and said hesitantly, 'I know it's not my place, but I feel you should know that Ahmed, Sultan Sadiq's aide, has been spreading rumours about you and Salman al Saqr…'

Jamilah flushed, mortification rising upwards. Stiffly she said, 'Thank you for letting me know.'

The woman walked out and Jamilah faced the mirror again. She sighed. No wonder people had been looking. She couldn't really blame the other man; that was effectively twice that Salman had upstaged him. But as of now her reputation was muck. Not that she was really worried about that; she wasn't bound by the same strictures as a lot of women from her part of the world. She had no family, and one of her parents had been European, so she'd always been something of an anomaly.

But it would be all over the place by the end of the day that she was sleeping with Salman, and he would have another very public notch to his bedpost.

She stood tall and smoothed her hair, before leaving the bathroom with her head held high. She had nothing to feel ashamed about except for her own very personal regret that she'd let herself be seduced by Salman all over again, despite all her lofty protestations.

'I have to go to a charity function tonight. I'd like you to come with me.'

Jamilah looked at Salman. He was dressed in a tuxedo again, and he'd been waiting for her when she got back to the suite. She was trying not to succumb to his intensely masculine pull—especially when she remembered the previous night. She was about to say no—she *wanted* to say no—and yet she hesitated. There was a quality to Salman's wide-legged stance which should have suggested power and authority, but which actually made Jamilah think of him as being vulnerable.

'What charity?'

Salman's face was unreadable. 'It's a charity I founded some years ago.'

Jamilah knew she couldn't stop the shock from registering on her face, and she saw Salman note it and smile cynically. 'You didn't have me down for a philanthropist, I see.'

Jamilah blanched at the fact that Salman was constantly surprising her with his multi-faceted personality, and got out something garbled, her curiosity well and truly ignited now, despite her best intentions.

'The charity is in someone else's name. They head it up publicly, and lobby for funding, but essentially it's my project.'

A thousand questions begged to be answered, but Jamilah held back. She couldn't not go now. 'Give me fifteen minutes and I'll be ready.'

Salman inclined his head and watched as Jamilah went to her bedroom. He'd actually been afraid she'd say no, and that realisation sent a feeling of nausea to his gut. He released a long breath, his heart hammering against his chest. He had no idea why he'd felt compelled to ask her. But some force had made him wait for her, and as soon as he'd seen her the words had spilled out. Frustration had been gnawing at his insides all day at being apart from Jamilah, and he didn't like it. Yet here he was, ensuring she be at his side for the whole evening and, more than that, witnessing him in a milieu that he'd never shared with anyone else. But then, he thought angrily, he'd spilled his guts to her only the other night, so why stop there?

The earth was shifting beneath his feet and he couldn't stop it. His desire for her burned even more fiercely now that it had been re-ignited, and in all honesty any woman he'd been with in the intervening six years was fading into an inconsequential haze.

He paced impatiently while he waited, and then he heard her. He turned around, already steeling himself against her effect, but it was no good. She was like a punch to his gut. A vision in a long swirling strapless dress of deep purple, which made her smokily made-up eyes pop out. Her hair was down around her shoulders.

Unable to stop himself, he walked over to her and cupped her jaw and cheek in one hand. He felt a delicate tremor run through her body, the hitch in her breath, and saw how her stunning eyes flared and darkened. Something exultant moved through him.

Words came up from somewhere deep inside him, and he had no more hope of holding them back than he would have of stopping an avalanche. 'You're mine, Jamilah.'

Her eyes narrowed, became mysterious. She was shutting herself off and he railed against it. 'And everyone knows it, Salman.' She smiled cynically. 'After your little theatrics last night we're the hot topic of the moment.'

Salman felt fire flare in his belly at the thought of that man touching Jamilah. He growled out now, 'Good. Because we're not finished yet, you and I.'

He bent his head and unerringly found her mouth. She resisted at first, but Salman used every sensual weapon in his arsenal until he could feel her curve softly towards him and her mouth opened on a delicious sigh. He plundered her sweet depths until she was clinging to him, and he was rock-hard and aching all over.

He pulled back and for a few seconds her eyes stayed closed, long lashes on flushed cheeks. He bit back a groan. But then her eyes flicked open and spat blue sparks at him. She trembled in his arms even as she said huskily, 'One more night, Salman. That's it. We go back to Merkazad tomorrow, and what we've had here is finished.'

Jamilah knew that after hearing the revelation of what Salman had endured as a child she wouldn't be able to keep up a façade of being unmoved while they made love for long. She longed to take him in her arms and comfort him, soothe his wounds, but he couldn't be making it any clearer that that was the last thing he needed or wanted.

Everything within Salman automatically rejected Jamilah's ultimatum, and yet he felt the desire to protect himself, feeling vulnerable for the second time in the space of mere minutes. First when he'd asked her to the function, and now this… Her ultimatum shouldn't be affecting him. He should be welcoming the prospect of his freedom. Hadn't he told her what to expect? Why shouldn't she want this to end? Any sane woman would…

He shrugged nonchalantly. 'If that's what you want…'

Her jaw tightened, and Salman longed to make it relax again, but Jamilah bit out, 'Yes, that's what I want. This ends here in Paris, for good.'

Anger and something much more ambiguous rose up around them as Salman reached for Jamilah's hand and took it. 'Fine. Well, let's get going, then. We don't want to miss a moment of our last night together.'

Our last night together. Even now, minutes later in the car, Jamilah had to struggle to beat back the prickle of tears. The realisation that she was still desperately in love with Salman was not so much a realisation as more a kind of resignation to her fate. How could she have thought for a second that she wasn't still in love with him? And, worse, falling even deeper all over again…

Her brave words that this would be finished in Paris still rang hollow in her head, because she knew it was just her pathetic attempt to make Salman think she was immune to him. She knew damn well that when they got back to Merkazad if he so much as touched her she'd be in his bed in a heartbeat. The only protection she could hope for was that if she went back to the stables and stayed there she'd be safe. Pathetic. She'd hide from him amongst the horses and take advantage of his fear, because she knew she wouldn't be able to trust herself to be near him. When she thought of that, she automatically wanted to help him get over his fear. *Pathetic*.

At that moment he took her hand and urged her towards him along the back seat of the car. His face was in shadow, all dark planes and sculpted lines, and she couldn't resist. When he bent his head and took her mouth in a soul-stealing kiss she gave herself up to the madness.

She was dizzy after Salman's thorough kisses by the time they reached a glittering hotel at the foot of the Champs-Elysées, and it was only when they were walking in that Jamilah realised Salman was nervous. He was gripping her hand. She looked up at him but his face was impassive.

An attractive middle-aged brunette was waiting to greet them in an immaculate dark suit. Salman introduced her to Jamilah as the co-ordinator of the charity. Their French was rapid, but Jamilah could keep up as she was fluent, too. The woman was explaining that everyone had just finished dinner and were ready to start listening to the speeches, and then an auction would take place. Salman nodded, and they followed the woman in through a side door and took a seat at a table near the front of the thronged ballroom.

Jamilah was aware of the way the energy in the room had zinged up a notch when people noted Salman's arrival, and of the intensely appreciative regard from women.

It was only when the speeches started that Jamilah realised which charity it was, and a jolt of recognition went through her. She'd read about it only recently when it had won a prestigious award. It was in aid of children who had suffered as a result of being drawn into conflict, and most especially for the notorious child soldiers of war-torn African countries. The charity was renowned for blazing a trail in setting up schools and psychological centres for those children, where they could go and be safe and get counselling to deal with their horrific experiences, with the view of either rehabilitating them with their families, if it was appropriate, or taking care of them till they could be independent.

Very few other charities offered such comprehensive, all-encompassing long-term care. No wonder Salman had set it up; he'd never had a chance of that kind of care to get over *his* wounds.

She watched dumbly as a young African man of about eighteen took to the podium. With heartbreaking eloquence he spoke of his experiences as a child soldier and how the charity had offered him life-saving solace. He was now living in Paris and attending the Sorbonne, having begun a law degree. By the time he'd finished talking Jamilah and many more in the auditorium had tears in their eyes. He got a standing ovation.

As he came off the podium he came straight over to Salman, who gave him a huge hug. He introduced the boy to Jamilah, who was too humbled to say anything more than a simple greeting. And then the crowd surrounded him and Salman sent him off with a wink. Jamilah could see how moved Salman was, too, with a curious light that she'd never seen before in his eyes.

He looked at her and she opened her mouth, questions and emotions roiling in her belly and her head. Still with that serious light in his eyes, he put a finger to her mouth and said enigmatically, while shaking his head,

'I don't want to talk about it—not tonight. But perhaps you can understand why I set it up…'

She could see the way his jaw had firmed, the determined glint in his dark eyes. She recognised his intractability. Eventually she nodded. And the obvious relief in his expression made her heart flip over in her chest. She'd just fallen a fathom deeper in love with Salman.

CHAPTER EIGHT

THEY stayed for the auction. Salman raised the bidding stakes by offering up a kiss from a well-known Hollywood heart-throb who was in the audience, and he bounded onto the stage, clearly loving the attention.

When it was over Salman tugged her up out of her seat and back through the side door. She looked at him as she tried to keep up, and asked a little breathlessly, 'Don't you have to…mingle or something?'

He looked back, eyes glittering. 'I employ people to do that for me. I extract the money, I run the charity anonymously, and I show my face every now and then.' He stopped in his tracks and turned so that Jamilah all but tumbled into his arms. 'Anyway,' he said throatily, 'I have a much more pressing engagement tonight.' With a subtle movement of his hips against hers she could feel exactly how *pressing* that engagement was.

She blushed, but forced herself to say, 'This is more important, though. I don't want to be responsible for taking you away…'

He silenced her words with a kiss, drawing her into a secluded alcove. People passed them by, but they were oblivious to everything but the heat between them. They finally came up for air and Jamilah groaned softly, resting her forehead on Salman's chest. Would she ever be free of this insanity?

When he took her hand again and led her out she was silent. Back in the car, she noticed that they weren't heading towards their hotel, and finally they pulled up at a small, slightly battered-looking restaurant boat that was moored near the Île de la Cité on the Seine. Lightbulbs were strung around the perimeter, bathing it in a golden glow. Her heart lurched. This had always been one of her favourite parts of Paris.

Salman led her down rickety steps and said, 'I thought you might be hungry...'

Jamilah's stomach growled, and she smiled. 'You seem to be more in tune with my eating habits than I am.'

He smiled, too, and for a second looked years younger—as if some of his dark intensity was lifting. She had to stem the rising tide of tenderness. Just then a rotund man came to the door and exclaimed over Salman effusively. Clearly he was a well-liked visitor. They were soon seated in a quiet corner, overlooking the slightly choppy river. The glowing lights of hundreds of apartments shone down on them, and on the water. Jamilah could see a couple on the path by the Seine stop and share a passionate kiss—it might have been her and Salman, six years ago. She sighed.

Salman took her hand and said lightly, 'You don't like this place?'

She shook her head and said quietly, avoiding his eye, 'It's perfect. I love it.' *And I love you. Still.* She curbed her words.

The waiter came then, to take their order, and Jamilah forced herself to relax. Salman ordered champagne and oysters, and they spoke of inconsequential things in an easy conversation that didn't stray anywhere near difficult topics. Jamilah could almost imagine for a second that she'd dreamt up Salman's horrific revelations…but then she only had to think of the charity and the work he was doing and remember.

By the time they had gorged on the succulent morsels, and after Salman had kissed and licked away the droplets that clung to her mouth, she was trembling with desire. When he stood up and took her hand to leave she didn't hesitate.

There was an ethereal quality to the silence between them as they travelled back to the hotel in the car, hand in hand. It lasted all the way up to their suite, and made Jamilah feel as if they were the only two people in the world.

Once they were in Salman's room, he took off his clothes with efficient gracefulness. Only once he was naked did he peel her dress down to expose her breasts and say throatily, 'I've been waiting to do this all night.'

With his hands on her waist he drew her into him, bent his head, and his hot mouth and tongue paid sensual homage to her breasts until she was gasping for air and her hips were squirming for more intimate contact.

When he had her naked on the bed, underneath him, he took her hands and lifted them over her head, capturing them there with one of his. He said, as he ran one hand down the side of her body, before his fingers sought the hot wet ache between her legs, 'I'm going to take this slowly…until you're begging for mercy…'

Jamilah whimpered as his fingers explored her moist heat and her hips bucked. She already felt like begging for mercy, but could only succumb to Salman's masterful seduction as he did exactly as he'd promised…

* * *

Jamilah had fallen into a sated drowsy slumber, but woke in an instant when she felt Salman brush her hair over one shoulder. He whispered in her ear. 'If you think this finishes here then you're very much mistaken, Jamilah Moreau.'

She said nothing—just felt a lump come into her throat. Salman settled himself around her, and eventually his breaths evened out. She knew he was right. She could no more resist him now than she could stop breathing and survive.

The only way she could make him reject her for sure would be to tell him how she felt. But the awful excoriating memory of that day six years before and the cruel rejection she'd suffered made her loath to reveal herself ever again. Even though she knew now that he hadn't *wanted* to hurt her.

Jamilah bit her lip. She had to batten down the fragile and fledgling flame of hope that rose up like a persistent desert flower in the face of certain demise once the rains had gone. She *had* to learn from the past. She would be the biggest fool on earth if she walked willingly back into Salman's arms once they returned to Merkazad. He'd only be there for another couple of weeks, and if she could just survive that long...

Next day, Salman cast a suspicious glance across the aisle of the private plane to Jamilah. Her chair was reclined and she was asleep—or she was pretending to be. Her face was turned away, and even that hint of obliviousness to his presence angered him. The minute they'd taken off she'd turned down the offer of lunch and yawned loudly. In all fairness he couldn't blame her. They hadn't got much sleep last night.

He tried to make sense of the tangled knot in his

head. He couldn't feel regret for having seduced Jamilah again—because it had felt too *right.* And now, as they flew back to the home he'd rejected a long time ago Merkazad was the last thing on his mind. To his surprise, he'd found himself enjoying the past few days, standing in for Nadim. They'd even managed to have a near-friendly conversation the previous evening, when Salman had filled him in on developments. And that was something that hadn't happened in a long time.

The woman sleeping so peacefully just a few feet away, *or not,* was the catalyst for these changes. Salman knew it, and it sent warning bells to every part of his body and brain. And yet he didn't regret telling her. If anything he felt guilty for burdening her with the images that had tortured his days and nights for years... He frowned; the images were already beginning to dissipate like wisps of cloud.

His mouth firmed and he turned away from the provocative sight of her tempting body. Resting his head back on the headrest, he closed his eyes. Things were different now from six years ago. Jamilah had matured and lived, had experienced things. He grimaced. She knew everything about him. But, despite that, he would be walking away and leaving her behind in Merkazad some day soon—and this time it really would be over. There simply was no other option.

'Stop the Jeep, Salman.'

When he didn't automatically obey, Jamilah was about to speak again, but then he did pull in. They were in the main courtyard of the Al-Saqr Castle. To the left the road led up to the castle, and to the right to the stables complex and training grounds.

Salman looked at Jamilah as she got out. 'Where do you think you're going?'

As nonchalantly as she could, while her heart was beating a rapid tattoo and every beat screamed to her, *coward, coward,* Jamilah said, 'Back to the stables, Salman. I'm going to be busy for the next few days, catching up.'

Salman jumped out of the Jeep so fast Jamilah's head swam. She instinctively moved away, but Salman cornered her at the back of the Jeep and caged her in with his hands by her head.

Dark eyes blistered down into hers, and she was instantly breathless. He ground his hips against hers and she could feel his arousal through his jeans, pressing her. 'So this is how it's to be? You run and hide at the stables?'

Jamilah tried to push him back, but he was immovable. She gritted out, trying to resist his magnetic pull, 'There's nothing stopping you coming with *me*—I have work to do, remember?'

Immediately he tensed, and Jamilah automatically wanted to say sorry when she saw the abject terror in the depths of his dark eyes. He pulled back and said coolly, 'Have it your way, then…we'll see how long you can last.'

He didn't have to say it. He wasn't prepared to deal with those demons. And, in all honesty, could she blame him? Even she felt sick when she thought of what he'd had to do. No wonder he'd escaped from here as soon as he'd had the chance.

Silently Jamilah told herself that she'd last until Salman was safely back in France and there were thousands of miles between them again. But as she watched him get back into the Jeep and drive away she had to fight back the treacherous feeling of disappointment that he hadn't tried harder to persuade her to go with him.

She turned and made the five-minute walk to the stables. When she arrived in the yard, which was normally her favourite place in the world, it suddenly felt cold and desolate and laden with malevolent images.

For the first day back in Merkazad at the stables Jamilah heard nothing from or about Salman—except the over-excited chatter of the girls who'd caught a glimpse of him that morning while they'd been exercising the horses. Jamilah wondered grumpily to herself where Abdul was when she needed him to nip that ardent gossiping in the bud.

By the time she fell into bed that evening, exhausted, she felt treacherously dissatisfied, wondering if Salman had lost interest after all. Perhaps he was going to import some of his hedonistic friends again to keep him amused?

Her dreams that night were hot and tangled, and she woke aching, and with an even bigger feeling of dissatisfaction.

Jamilah groaned as she got up for work. This was after only one day? She was a lost cause.

Around mid-morning, one of the castle maids appeared, and handed Jamilah a note in a blank envelope. With her heart skittering ominously, she turned away to read it. The slashing confident scrawl was instantly familiar.

Was yesterday as hard for you as it was for me?
I want you, Jamilah…

Jamilah dismissed the girl, who'd obviously been waiting to see if she wanted to send a reply, and it took her a couple of hours to get over the note and its sheer audacity. It also took her that long to quiet down the tumult of emotions the note had provoked: relief that Salman hadn't forgotten about her, anger at herself for feeling like a lovestruck teenager, anger that he was intent on pursuing the affair despite her declaration in Paris, and anger at her body's clamour to give in.

Just as she was thinking that, her mobile phone beeped. Jamilah opened the text. *Did you get my note?* it read. After a moment of deliberation Jamilah replied. *Yes. Not interested in pursuing this topic of conversation. I am very busy.*

She got another one back almost instantly. *I'm busy, too. In case it's escaped your attention I'm the acting ruler of Merkazad. Yet I can't seem to concentrate.*

Jamilah found she was smiling, and had to stop and rearrange her facial muscles. She resolutely turned her phone off and got back to work. But as the day progressed a flurry of envelopes kept arriving via staff from the castle. And they all contained increasingly explicit notes about Salman's varying states of arousal, what he imagined she might be wearing, how he wanted to remove it, and what he wanted to do to her once he had removed it.

By the end of the day Jamilah was over-hot and over-wrought, but refused to give in to the pull to go and confront Salman directly and tell him to lay off. That was no doubt exactly what he wanted, and in the semi-aroused state she was in there was no way she'd be able to resist him if he tried to seduce her.

The stables were her only hope of sanctuary, and she hated that she was using them as protection.

The following day the same pattern emerged. Note after note. Her phone beeping constantly even though she deleted his messages now, without reading them. He was driving her insane. She amended that. She was driving herself insane. But only because she couldn't stop thinking about what he was saying and reacting to it.

Are you hot right now? Are you thinking of that shower we had together in Paris? Where do you ache most?

It was a sensual attack for which Jamilah was woefully unprepared. And that night, when her phone rang by her bed, she snatched it up and said irritably, 'Yes?'

She heard a dark chuckle. 'Why so grumpy? Can't you sleep? Too hot?'

Jamilah gripped the phone hard in a suddenly sweaty palm, acutely aware of how hot she did feel in her small T-shirt and panties. She forced herself to sound as cool as she could. 'Not at all. Unlike you, I've been extremely busy.'

Another chuckle floated down the line, and Salman said with a mock self-effacing tone, 'Luckily I possess above average intelligence, so I find multi-tasking very easy. Although writing those notes *was* having an adverse affect on me while I conducted a public meeting in Merkazad.'

Jamilah had to stifle a giggle at the thought of Salman becoming aroused and trying to hide it, and then the giggle died when she realised that the thought was making her aroused. She couldn't believe it; they were no better than teenagers. She squirmed and pressed her legs together, aghast that he could have this effect on her down a phone line.

'Are you in bed now?'

'No.' Jamilah immediately lied.

'Liar,' Salman chided huskily. 'What are you wearing?'

'Seeing as how I'm not in bed, I'm wearing jeans and a shirt.'

'Like I said: liar. Let me guess. You're a small T-shirt and panties girl? That is when you're not naked with me.'

Jamilah squirmed again. 'No, actually. I wear pyjamas buttoned from top to toe.'

He made a tsk-tsk sound. 'At this rate you'll be going straight to hell, Jamilah Moreau.'

Quickly she quipped, 'Sounds like it'll be a bit overcrowded, with you there, too.'

'Touché.' That hint of bleakness in his voice sounded down the line, and Jamilah instantly felt chastened. But she didn't have time to think about it because he was saying, 'Do you know what I'm thinking of right now?'

More huskily than she wanted, she said, 'I don't think I really want to know, Salman. In fact I'm quite tired—'

He cut her off. 'I'm thinking about you lying there with your hair spread out, in a T-shirt which reveals your midriff and exquisitely shaped waist and hips. I'm thinking of how it's stretched tight across your breasts, and how your pants cling to your hips. I'm thinking of how I'd like to pull your T-shirt up so that I can bare your breasts to my gaze, see how your nipples harden and pout for my touch, for my tongue…'

'Salman…' Jamilah said weakly, as a liquid heat invaded her veins. Her hand was on her belly, and of its own volition was sliding down towards her pants.

'Salman, what?' he asked huskily. 'Stop? You don't want me to stop. You want me there, to suckle on your breasts until your back is arched, while my hand descends to spread your thighs apart, before coming back up to slide aside your pants and explore, to find where you're so wet and aching…'

It was Jamilah's own hand almost touching the spot he spoke of that brought her back to cold reality. She jackknifed off the bed and slammed the phone down into its cradle. When it rang again almost immediately she yanked the cord out of the wall.

And only when the waves of heat began to subside did she manage to fall into a fitful sleep.

The following day Jamilah was clinging onto her resolve, which felt like a flimsy life raft in a choppy sea. More notes had arrived that morning, but Jamilah couldn't even look at them now. She sent them back unopened to Salman, with the bemused maids.

So later that day, when she heard the arrival of a Jeep in the main stable courtyard, she whirled around, heart thudding ominously. *He'd come—he wanted her so badly that he'd come to get her.* And treacherously her resolve was already dissolving fast.

Salman stepped out of the Jeep and she felt weak with longing. He was tall and dark and she felt as if she hadn't seen him in months. And the look on his face was so determined it made her tremble all over.

But she couldn't give in. She couldn't.

He just stood there for a long moment. An unspoken dialogue hummed between them. Finally he articulated it. 'Come up to the castle with me, Jamilah.'

She shook her head and backed away, even as every cell in her body was urging her to go with him. At that moment one of the stablehands led a horse out of a stall just a few feet away. She saw how Salman's eyes veered wildly to the horse and then back to her.

He'd gone deathly pale in the space of a heartbeat, and he gritted out, 'Damn you, Jamilah. I'm not ready for this.'

And then he was back in his Jeep and screeching out of the stableyard, and she felt as if she'd just done something unutterably cruel. For the first time since she'd seen him again she got a sense that she had the power to hurt him, and it made her reel.

She was still standing there, slightly stunned, when she noticed Abdul by one of the stables. He just looked at her, and then shook his head slowly, and Jamilah felt even worse.

She barely slept a wink that night; not surprisingly there had been no more notes or phone calls from Salman after he'd left. Her head was whirling with guilt and her resolve not to give in to the almost overpowering pull to go to Salman.

She started work in a daze the next day, and was exhausted by four p.m., when the phone rang in her office.

It was a call that made her want to weep with weariness, for it meant that she had to take the chopper to a remote Bedouin oasis village, deep in a mountainous valley. Considering the time of day it was, and the way Bedouin hospitality worked, she'd more than likely have to stay overnight.

Apparently a horse was having trouble foaling, and its owner feared for its life and that of the foal. The stables' resident vet was away for a few days, and Jamilah had studied veterinary science, so she had the necessary expertise when things like this cropped up from time to time. She gathered her things and called the chopper pilot, then made her way to the launching pad behind the castle. As she drove by the castle she resolutely veered her mind away from the man inside…*somewhere*.

They flew over mountainous and rocky terrain, and Jamilah's heart clenched with emotion for this sometimes inhospitable country. It was these local Bedouin people who had risen up and fought back against the invaders all those years before, who had saved the Sheikh and his family from their incarceration. *Who had saved Salman.*

Jamilah could see the village now, down far below in the crevasse of a deep valley. Mountain springs kept it verdant and lush, and it was like a tiny green pocket of paradise within a lunar landscape. It was only as they got closer that Jamilah saw a Jeep waiting and felt the first prickle of suspicion, but she told herself she was being ridiculous.

When she got out a driver was waiting, and he helped her into the Jeep. They were heading for the village, but she couldn't see any villagers, or any children waiting for their treats which she always brought. She reassured herself that it was late, dusk was closing in. These valley people were traditional and had probably retired for the night.

But before they got to the village itself Jamilah saw a tent set up by a palm tree and a picturesque pool, set back in its own enclosure. It was the kind of tent that was set up for Nadim whenever he travelled into the country. Her skin prickled ominously when the driver stopped the Jeep outside it. She got out, and at that moment heard the helicopter taking off into the distance.

Before she had a chance to register the significance of

that, someone stepped out of the tent. Someone tall and dark and imposing, dressed in ceremonial Merkazadi robes. As if she didn't already know...*Salman*.

CHAPTER NINE

THE jeep was already turning around and heading away. Jamilah stared at Salman, and an awful yearning rushed through her. Even though she'd seen him just the day before, she'd *missed* him. And a wild excitement was making the blood rush through her veins. She wanted to walk up to Salman and hit him and kiss him all at the same time. The sheer gall of his gesture made her breathless, but its sheer romanticism made her weak with longing.

Damned if she was going to let him know. She had to resist him—*had* to. For, as surely as night followed day, he intended to walk away from her again and she would never get over him. Not now. How could she when she now knew the secret behind his dark essence? His vulnerability?

She hitched her bag on her shoulder, eyes spitting blue sparks at him, and Salman felt curiously weak for a moment. Jamilah had never looked so beautiful. In worn jeans, a shirt and boots, no make-up, and her hair slipping out of its ponytail to curl in long dark silky tendrils around her face. Since he'd seen her last it had felt like a century.

She hitched up her chin and said frostily, 'I presume that there is no horse in labour?'

He shook his head, jaw clenched, and folded his arms.

'So you're kidnapping people now? Pretty inventive for a hedge fund manager. But really you should save your ingenuity for someone who wants to be kidnapped by you.'

Salman's insides clenched at her blistering tone, her obvious reluctance to be here, but he couldn't let her walk away. He needed her too badly.

Jamilah turned and started to walk away, into the village. 'I'm going to get a horse and ride back to Merkazad if I have to. It'll only take a day or two.'

She was grabbed from behind, her bag falling to the ground, and before she could emit a squeak of protest Salman had carried her bodily into the tent, which was lit with a hundred small lamps, imbuing the luxuriously furnished surroundings with a decadent feel. And right in the middle of the tent stood a low divan, covered in satins and silken throws. It was a seduction scene straight out of a movie.

He put her down and she whirled around, feeling her hair come undone completely. '*Will* you stop doing that!'

Her heart was careening wildly against her breastbone, but Salman just said calmly, 'The chopper will come back in three days. As will the Jeep. And you won't attempt to get a horse from any of the locals as they've been instructed not to let you have one.'

Three days!

Shock and something much more like panic made Jamilah say shakily, 'Why on earth would you want to isolate us here for three days?'

Salman's jaw clenched. 'Because you've denied us

three days by your theatrics, refusing to come back to the castle.'

Guilt lanced her at her own cowardly behaviour even as she said cuttingly, 'I run the stables, Salman. It's hardly *theatrics* to want to be near to where I work. That's where I live.' Sheer panic that he could wield such control over her and her emotions made her lash out unthinkingly, 'And could you *be* any further from the stables here?'

Salman paled in an instant, and immediately the words were out Jamilah felt contrite. He stepped back and she put out a hand. 'Salman, I'm sorry. I shouldn't have said that.'

He backed away, and conversely Jamilah wanted to pull him to her. He ran a hand through his hair and laughed curtly, harshly. 'You're right, though. It's pathetic. I couldn't even last a minute in that place.'

Jamilah walked up to Salman and took his hand. She said softly, all rancour gone, 'No one could blame you—not after what you were forced to do there.'

He looked down at her, his eyes two pools of dark shadows. 'I don't know if I prefer you spitting and hissing and resisting me or like this, full of pity.'

Jamilah shook her head, her hair slipping over one shoulder. 'I don't pity you, Salman. It's not pity…it's empathy.'

He lowered his head and pressed his lips to hers. Feeling completely exposed, Jamilah couldn't help but respond, and flames of passion were not far behind. When the kiss was fast developing into something much more urgent and carnal Jamilah somehow found the strength to pull away. Breathing harshly, she put her hands on Salman's chest and leaned back. 'I won't do this, Salman. I told you in Paris that it was over. I won't be your convenient plaything just because I'm here and it's easy.'

In two seconds he had taken Jamilah's face in his hands. His mouth swooped down on hers again, all softness gone, hard and hot and demanding. She could feel his straining body move sinuously against hers and had to lock her hips to stop herself from responding. Damn him—and her immediate response. She finally wrenched her mouth away. Her hands were still fists on his chest between them.

'Does that feel easy to you?' he demanded throatily.

'You can't use sex to avoid questions, Salman al Saqr, and I will not stay here with you for three days.'

'Believe me, if you showed no signs of wanting me then I would have no problem leaving you alone. Women who don't find me desirable have never turned me on.'

Jamilah could have laughed—as if such a woman existed!

'So…what? You've put a time limit on this desire? Is that it? Three days and we will have exhausted ourselves and burnt it out?' Even the thought of three days indulging in such a thing made her quiver inside.

Salman smiled and it was wolfish, sending skitters of anticipation down Jamilah's spine. 'In three days I'm hoping that we will be exhausted, yes. And perhaps some semblance of sanity will be restored—because one thing is certain: I haven't felt sane where you're concerned for a long time.'

It was suddenly important for her to know something. 'That night…the night in Paris six years ago…did you go out with that woman as you said you were going to?' Even now the poisonous image of the red-headed siren inserted itself with savage vividness into Jamilah's brain.

Salman slowly shook his head, and his hands relaxed a little on her face. She could feel him brush a lock of hair away from her cheek. His body was still welded to hers and his arousal was insistent. 'No...I never saw her again—except through work. And, believe me, she didn't take kindly to being let down.' His mouth thinned, as if it pained him to be admitting this. 'I actually went out that night and got blind drunk. The one and only time in my life.'

Jamilah pushed herself free of his hold and stepped away, turning around so he couldn't see her face. Emotions erupted in her chest. She knew he wouldn't just say this, knew that he would not lie—why would he need to? He'd been crueller than anyone she'd ever known, so why wouldn't he hesitate to give her the truth if he *had* slept with her? This revelation was inserting itself into a very vulnerable part of her, smashing aside another piece of the wall she'd erected around herself to keep out all hurt and feeling. He kept doing this—kept turning her memories of what had happened in Paris on their head, telling her that there had been so much more to it than the banal yet cruel rejection that had fed her anger for so long.

And she hated him for it, because she was sure that it cost him nothing to admit this. That he was completely unaware how seismic this admission was to her. She whirled back around to face him, willing herself to be strong.

'I won't give you three days, Salman. I feel sane enough for the both of us, believe me. This is pure indulgence on your part. You're bored and frustrated because for once in your life you're not getting what you want and you simply can't handle it.'

He moved towards her, and with big hands closing around her waist he pulled her to him. She could see anger flare in his eyes at her defiance. 'Your refusal to see me as anything but a feckless, petulant playboy is growing wearisome, Jamilah. This goes far deeper than such superficial emotions, believe me.'

She stood stiff in his embrace. But her conscience struck her. She knew well that she could no longer label him as such. He was far from the shallow playboy everyone believed him to be. She threw her head back, determined not to let herself succumb to the three days of bliss she knew only he could promise. It would be all too easy for her to hope for more, to believe that perhaps things were different this time round.

She ignored the provocative sight of the luxurious bed nearby. 'Well, what else am I supposed to think when you use your powerful position to get what you want?'

Her words struck Salman somewhere deep inside, and he fought not to let the emotion she aroused to show on his face. But the fact was this: he'd never had to go to so much trouble to get a woman into his bed before. He'd never been so consumed by a woman. His heart beat hard; that wasn't true. He had once before, and it had been *this* woman.

There'd never been a moment when she hadn't occupied some corner of his mind, when he hadn't been aware of her. He could see that now. Growing up, he'd felt guilty as a young man, being so aware of how her young, firm body had been developing and maturing. The day he'd left Merkazad she'd been sixteen years old and he'd touched her cheek, when in actual fact he'd had to battle a desire to kiss her.

'I want you, Jamilah. That's all that matters here. We're alone. Miles away from civilisation.'

He couldn't know how seductive those words were—how many times she'd woken from hot and tangled dreams in which he'd come back to Merkazad and whisked her away for exactly such illicit pleasure.

Suddenly sounding eminently reasonable, and not at all passionate, Salman stepped away and said, 'Night has fallen outside.'

Jamilah blinked stupidly, and could see through the gap in the lavish drapes that night had indeed fallen. Stars twinkled in a clear sky and a half moon glistened. Night creatures filled the air with their chirrups and sounds. And she hadn't even noticed.

'You must be tired and hungry. Why don't you wash and we'll eat?'

He said this as if he hadn't all but kidnapped her—as if they were not in some remote and magical part of Merkazad—but as if this were entirely normal. She watched as he walked over to the far side of the tent and picked up a gold-embossed box. He put it on the bed and turned to her, saying with a rough quality to his voice, 'I brought you some things to wear.'

The audacity of his statement made her melt inside while it also stiffened her resolve not to give in to this arrogant and autocratic game of his. 'I won't be wearing any clothes other than my own, Salman. This is ridiculous. I'm not your mistress.'

Her mouth thinned. 'But I am hungry, and I am tired. And clearly I'm stuck here for the night now. I'll wash and eat, and then I'm going to bed—*alone*. In my own clothes.' Belligerently she said, as she got her bag and made for the curtained-off washing area, 'I don't know where *you're* going to sleep tonight, but the least you can do is let me have the tent.'

Salman's eyes flashed, and she thought she saw his mouth quirk as if she amused him, but before she could respond to the fresh anger mixed with panic spiking within her he said smoothly, 'I'll arrange for one of the girls to come and help you, and for dinner to be served.'

Jamilah shut her mouth and all but fled to the washing area, which was lit with the light of a hundred gently flickering candles. Her heart ached in her chest as she was momentarily transfixed by the scene. In any other circumstance she would long for just this scenario. It came fully formed out of her fantasies. But not now, and not like this, with *this* man. And yet…her heart ached even harder…with *who else?*

He might want three more days with her, but what else might he demand? He wasn't done with her. And she certainly wasn't done with him. And yet all this fighting her response to him was exhausting. His notes and that incendiary phone call had taken a lot more out of her than she wanted to admit to.

Just then she heard a sound, and a young, shy Bedouin girl came in, dressed from head to toe in black. She started filling the ornate bath and gave Jamilah a robe to change into. Jamilah was aware of the feminine ritual even though she'd never been indulged like this before. This kind of thing was usually reserved for members of the ruling family—the Sheikha and the Sheikh's mistresses.

Her blood ran cold. *Was* she Salman's mistress now?

For this was exactly how a mistress was treated, wasn't it? Flown in to meet him, bought clothes, wined and dined, washed and readied for his pleasure. Disgust curled low in her belly even as something much more treacherous made her blood grow hot. There was something so inherently decadent and sexy about this ritual, and it called to a deeply secret feminine part of herself that she'd never acknowledged before. She hated to admit that.

The girl had prepared the bath, and the scent of exotic oils rose to make Jamilah's skin tingle all over. She stripped and put on the robe, barely noticing when the girl took her bundle of clothes away and said she'd be back presently. Too seduced not to be able to respond, Jamilah groaned softly as she slid into the perfumed satiny water. She never indulged herself like this. For such a long time she'd subjugated any kind of feminine luxury. For a second she forgot her tangled emotions and her anger at Salman: this was pure bliss…

Salman had come back into the tent momentarily, to see that the dinner preparations were being made to his specifications. He'd been pacing while staff scurried in and out. Now they were gone while they prepared the hot food. He heard the gentle movement of the bath water in the curtained-off corner of the dimly lit tent, and to imagine Jamilah there now, naked, was almost more than he could bear.

Knowing he shouldn't, but unable to help himself, he walked over to the screen. He could hear her soft moan of pleasure, the splash of water, and his body tightened unbearably. Through a chink in the screen he became transfixed when he saw slivers of Jamilah's body—the swell of her pale olive-skinned breasts with those dusky nipples. Her elegant shoulders. A tendril of wet hair sloping down to one bountiful curve.

Jamilah stilled in the water for a moment, soap between her hands. Someone was watching her. She could feel it. But she couldn't call out. She felt a kind of paralysis grip her, and suddenly didn't want to break the spell that seemed to be weaving itself around her. She knew it was Salman. She could sense his presence a mile away. And to know that he was watching her through the screen, illicitly, was the most erotic thing she'd ever felt.

Suddenly she had power in her hands. She had *him* at a disadvantage. She knew there was no way he'd come to her like this, while they might be caught, but still she could sense his eyes on her in this secret and brief moment. With a hitherto non-existent feminine pride and confidence she soaped her body, trailing her hands up each arm luxuriously, before soaping her shoulders.

With her eyes half closed she washed her breasts, and imagining Salman watching sent her arousal into orbit. Her nipples were already tight and hard, and when she ran her hands over them she couldn't stop the faintest mewling sound coming from her throat. She was meant to be teasing *him,* not herself, and yet…she couldn't stop.

His provocative notes from the past few days came back to her: *Do you touch yourself when you think about me? Are you hot now? Are you wet and aching for me? I dreamt of you last night and woke up hard, wanting you…*

Unaware of the spell she was binding around herself, Jamilah let her fingers trap one nipple, squeezing the hard peak so that a flame burst to life in her belly. Her other hand drifted down over her belly, under the water, to between her legs. To where the water lapped against her hot and slippery flesh.

It was only when she heard something that sounded like a strangled moan and then more noises that she came out of her sensual reverie, shooting up to sit in the bath, suddenly mortified and burning up all over. What had just happened to her? She'd been as good as starring in her own X-rated video! And all because she'd thought Salman had been watching. He probably hadn't been—it could have been anyone! *Oh, God,* Jamilah thought, what had she turned into?

Just then she heard the girl return, and Jamilah practically jumped out of the bath, grabbing the towel out of the girl's hands. Too mortified to look the young girl in the eye, she hunted around for her clothes, but they and her bag were gone. She asked the girl where they were and she blushed prettily, saying that the Sheikh had told her to wash Jamilah's clothes and to give *him* her bag. She said, 'The Sheikh has left some clothes for you...' Immediately Jamilah thought of that glossy box and its connotations.

When the maid indicated to Jamilah where there was an array of scents and body lotions, Jamilah said, more curtly than she'd intended, 'I don't need any of that. I just want my own clothes.'

A tortured expression crossed the girl's face, and immediately Jamilah felt contrite. She was only following orders, and in this rural milieu you absolutely did not question the demands of the Sheikh. Jamilah apologised and gave in, knowing she couldn't do anything else for the moment, 'Thank you for the bath, and the lotions... but I can do that myself. Why don't you bring the clothes you've been left in here, so I can get changed?'

While the relieved girl was gone, Jamilah picked up the nearest lotion and smoothed it on as perfunctorily as she could, trying to ignore its heady musky scent and the way her skin tingled to her touch. When the girl came back, looking much happier, Jamilah didn't have the heart to say anything more about her own things. She would work on getting them back some other way.

But when the girl opened up the big glossy box with unmistakable reverence, and pulled out a long kaftan-style dress which seemed to be made entirely out of spun silver, Jamilah gasped, transfixed.

The girl said in awe, 'It is beautiful, is it not?'

Jamilah touched it. 'Yes, very.' It looked as if it had been made by fairies—a human hand too clumsy for something so ethereal. When it moved, glints of dark blue thread shone like bursts of sapphire.

And with it came underwear made of lace so delicate it looked as if it would fall apart at a mere touch. The royal blue colour made the pale olive of her skin stand out, and to Jamilah's constant embarrassment her nipples stiffened against the delicate lace, as if it were a lover's touch. She hated that she was getting dressed to Salman's specifications. She hated that she was falling in with his plans. Even as a secret part of her felt the insidious slow curling, burning of desire which, once started, would not rest until it had been sated.

Once Jamilah was dressed, with the kaftan lovingly clinging to her every curve, the maid brushed her hair until it too shone like spun black silk. Eventually, when her nerves were screaming with tension, the girl was finished, and with downbent gaze she left.

Taking a deep breath, Jamilah emerged from behind the screen to see Salman's broad-shouldered powerful physique dominating the doorway of the tent. Instantly her insides contracted with a pulsing of pleasure she couldn't stop. She gritted her jaw and her hands went to fists by her sides.

She couldn't make out Salman's expression; he was too far away and in the shadows, and all she could think about was how she'd felt him watching her and how she'd touched herself so wantonly. If it even *had* been him! Liquid heat moistened her still sensitive sex.

And then abruptly, breaking the moment of tension, Salman strode in. The curtains closed heavily behind him and they were cocooned in this lavish tent, in a remote oasis in the far eastern reaches of Merkazad.

He stood tall and resplendent in Merkazadi robes by a table which had been laid and was now heaving with succulent-looking food. The smells alone were more enticing than anything she'd ever experienced before, and Jamilah firmly pushed aside the implication that it was because it was *here,* with *him.* Because he had done this for her.

On shaky legs she walked over, her stomach growling with hunger all of a sudden. She refused to meet Salman's eyes as she approached the table, acutely self-aware in the dress, and she would have kept avoiding his eye if he hadn't caught her arm in a burning grip and with his other hand tipped her chin up so that she had to look at him.

Roughly he said, 'You are more beautiful tonight than I've ever seen you.'

Jamilah bristled when heady pleasure suffused her body at his statement. She tried to block out how gorgeous *he* was, with a faint line of stubble accentuating his hard jaw, the robes making him look so effortlessly regal and powerful. 'Well, I hope it's worth it, after all the trouble and expense you've gone to, to get me out here.'

'It'll be worth it, Jamilah,' he promised. 'And the pleasure won't be mine alone. I'll make sure of that.'

Reacting to that promise, and feeling shrewish, she said, 'Well, you can save me the sordid details of whose pleasure it will be, because you won't be sharing *my* bed tonight, Salman.'

He chuckled softly and let her go, indicating for her to sit down. His easy laughter made her want to bounce something off his head, but Jamilah clenched her jaw and sat down, feeling very huffy and petulant. Alien moods for her—she was usually so calm and controlled.

It was a struggle for Salman to appear urbane as Jamilah sat down opposite him, refusing to meet his eye. He was harder than he'd ever been in his life, thanks to that little X-rated water show she'd put on. Only the return of the staff to prepare for dinner had stopped him from smashing aside the screen so that he could strip and lower himself into that bath, embed himself between her glorious legs and take her so hard and fast their heads would have been spinning for a week.

And that dress… It covered her almost as comprehensively as the ubiquitous shirts and jeans she wore, but it shimmered and clung to dips and hollows with a sensuality that made him grit his jaw and curl his hands into fists to stop himself from reaching out to touch her.

She sent him a skittish little glance, and he saw a pulse beat hectically at the base of her neck. Dark triumph filled him. She could fight this—*him*—until she was blue in the face, but ultimately she wouldn't be able to deny her own desire. But for now he forced himself to take control of his libido, and put a plate of different morsels of food together for her.

Jamilah took the plate Salman handed her, seeing that he had automatically picked all of her favourite foods. Her heart clenched. And then she saw him pour them *both* some champagne. She quirked a brow in his direction, striving not to remember how it had felt to learn that she'd been the cause of his one lapse of control with alcohol. That he hadn't been unmoved by his actions after all…

He smiled and held up his glass, 'To us, Jamilah.'

She smiled back sweetly and clinked her glass with his. 'To *me,* and the good night's sleep I'm going to have in this lovely tent, all on my own.'

He chuckled again and drank from his glass, and Jamilah's eyes were momentarily transfixed by the powerful bronzed column of his throat. Tearing her gaze away, hating the flush of awareness climbing up her body, she ate—and nearly choked on a plump, succulent prawn when Salman said lazily, 'I enjoyed our correspondence over the last few days—even if it was a little one-sided, and did leave me somewhat…unsatisfied.'

Jamilah wiped at her mouth with a napkin. She might have thrown the notes away in disgust, but not until after she'd read most of them with a guilty pleasure. Which Salman had honed in on as soon as they'd spoken on the phone. And she might have slammed the phone down on him, but she hadn't been able to get him out of her head. She hadn't been far off touching herself, just as she had in the bath earlier, and she squirmed to remember that now.

Salman caught her hand across the table, and her gaze skittered to his guiltily.

'Were you thinking of me just now…in the bath? You must have known I was watching…'

Enthralled and mesmerised, Jamilah could say or do nothing. To agree would mean that she couldn't turn back from him tonight, because he'd know that he'd turned her on with little more than the thought that he'd been there. In a strangled voice she said shakily, 'I don't know what you're talking about.'

He quirked a hard smile. 'I told you once before I admired your honesty. Lying doesn't suit you.'

Jamilah pulled her hand free and continued eating, even though her appetite had spectacularly fled. She was burning up from the inside out. Very aware of Salman lazily feeding himself, imagining his tongue snaking out to catch the juices from his morsels of food, just as hers had to do.

But, save running out of the tent and causing a furore by seeking sanctuary with one of the village folk, she was stuck. She didn't know or care where Salman would go tonight, as long as he wasn't here, but she had a sinking feeling that he'd made no such alternative preparation, despite her assertion.

She put down her napkin and finished the last droplets of sparkling liquid in her heavy glass. The sheer opulence of this whole scene stunned her anew, and she wondered how Salman had got everything here and prepared. She quashed her curiosity, affected a yawn, and stood up, ready to restate her intention to sleep alone.

Salman stood smoothly on the other side of the table and held out a hand, which Jamilah predictably ignored. Salman quashed the dart of anger and frustration. 'You know I'm not going anywhere, Jamilah.'

She looked at him, and underneath the defiance he saw something else—something infinitely more vulnerable that he hardened his heart to. He didn't want to deal with that. He just wanted Jamilah. And she wanted him. That was all he needed to know.

He walked over to the sumptuous bed and started to disrobe.

'What are you doing?' Jamilah's voice came out as a panicked squeak, and she cursed herself for not sounding more in control.

Salman turned around, supremely confident. 'I'm getting ready for bed.'

'But where will *I* go?'

He indicated with a hand. 'There's a perfectly good bed right here.'

'Yes,' Jamilah hissed, 'but not while you're in it.'

Salman ignored her, and turned away to continue disrobing. In the light of the hundreds of small glowing lamps, bit by bit his impressive body was revealed. And Jamilah could only stand and watch, until he stood there with his back to her, long, lean and powerful. And gorgeous enough to make her throat dry. His back was impossibly broad, and led down to the taut muscular globes of his bottom, and heavily muscled powerful legs.

It felt like the hardest equation in the world to work out why she had to get out of there so badly. And then he slowly turned around, and her world contracted to this tiny spot on the planet and this tent. And this man and this desire thrumming between them. The air seemed to be hotter, redolent with scents and whispered desires.

'Jamilah…'

Jamilah was finding it hard to raise her gaze from where it had dropped to take in his impressive erection. A pulse beat through her blood with gathering force.

And as she watched, and faintly heard Salman groan, he wrapped a hand around himself, as if unable *not* to.

Her legs nearly buckled at the sight of his hand moving back and forth slowly, how the silky skin slipped up and down over the strong shaft and, worse, she could imagine how it felt and was jealous.

'*Jamilah*…you're torturing me. I need you.'

Her gaze lifted with an effort. She felt all at once heady, languorous and energised. It was a combination that had her insides fizzing. But even as she felt her traitorous feet move towards Salman she shook her head, struggling to make a stand, not to give in.

'I…I can't. I won't do this. I can't do this again with you, Salman.'

On a broken sob which was torn from deep in her chest she turned around to block out the provocative view, to block out temptation. She was shaking all over with reaction, and just knew that if Salman succeeded she would never have a chance to get over him.

Big hands settled on her shaking shoulders with surprising gentleness and turned her around. To her chagrin she could feel tears prick her eyes, threatening to overflow.

Salman sounded tortured. 'Please, Jamilah, don't cry…'

A vivid memory of that day by their parents' graves struck Jamilah then. How Salman had told her not to cry, to be strong. She looked up at him, past and present morphing into one. Her heart beat fast. She loved him. She loved this man with an intensity that eclipsed anything she might have felt before. And it was already way too late to be saved or helped.

As the tears overflowed and slid down her cheeks at the acknowledgement of that truth, she felt something give way inside herself. How could she walk away from this now? When perhaps this was all she would have to remember? This oasis in the rocky desert, this moment in time…

Salman's face looked tortured, his eyes dark with some emotion that made her head reel; it was an emotion he hadn't revealed before. He said gutturally, 'I won't make you do this if it's going to upset you so much. I never wanted to upset you. I just thought you wanted me as much as I want you…but were fighting it to pay me back…because you know how much I need you.'

His tenderness undid her completely, and the fact that he wasn't being autocratic, wasn't forcing her, made her even weaker against his pull. She trusted him. She trusted that he actually meant what he said—that if she were to ask him to leave her alone he would. He'd walk out of there and let her have the tent to herself. Suddenly it was the last thing she wanted.

This was what she'd been afraid of—that it would be impossible to resist him now that she knew his deepest darkest self, because she ached so much to take that pain away. Jamilah shook her head on a reflex. He believed that she'd been trying to get some sort of revenge on him? That *that* had been behind her reluctance to continue the affair? She shook her head again, and put her hands up to Salman's face and jaw, caressing him. His breath hitched and his body tensed.

'No. That's not what I was doing, Salman. But I don't care about that any more. I don't care about anything but right here and now, and I can't keep resisting.'

She pressed close, so that she could feel his erection hard between them. 'Make love to me, Salman. I need you so much.'

He waited for a long moment, as if expecting her to

laugh in his face, tell him she hadn't meant it, and then with a growl of triumph his head swooped down and his mouth burnt hers in a searing brand. His arms wrapped tight around her and triumph coursed through Jamilah too, as if the two warring sides of her psyche had battled it out and the stronger side had finally won. She knew in some dim place that she would have to deal with the fallout of this decision, but not right now.

Right now she needed Salman with a pulsing intensity she'd never felt before. And the vulnerable chink he'd just shown her was the most powerful aphrodisiac in the world.

With one swoop he smashed aside all her resistance, lifted her up and carried her over to the bed, where he laid her down as if she was the most infinitely delicate and precious thing in the world...

A couple of hours later Salman was lying on the silken sheets, wide awake, with Jamilah's hair in a silken caress over his chest and her breasts pressing into his side. One arm was wrapped around her, holding her to him, his fingers near the enticing swell of her breast. Even though he'd never felt more sated in his life, his body was already responding with predictable force. He sighed deeply.

Jamilah had capitulated, but it didn't make him feel triumphant or complacent. He'd never known such an unremitting hunger for one woman. The more he got of Jamilah, the more he wanted. And it sent tentacles of faint panic through him. Because how could he leave and get on with his life when Jamilah's life was here? Seeing her tears earlier had been like a punch in the gut. He knew he shouldn't have pushed her—knew he shouldn't have brought her here. But he was weak, and he needed her, and the depth of that need stunned him.

He refused to believe that his need had grown more acute since the night he'd spilled his guts in Paris, but he was very much afraid that was the case. She was the only person he'd ever told about what had happened to him, and yet his fear of how she might have used that knowledge was eclipsed by this insatiable desire. And of *course* she hadn't used the knowledge.

Jamilah was a slice of sun he was indulging in, and he knew he was on a finite time with her—because she would want a *normal* life. With someone who didn't harbour the worst images of degradation and pain. How could she not? His heart clenched ominously when he thought of the children she would have with someone else, and he quashed the scary yearning feeling that rose up.

When he felt a telling change in Jamilah's breathing across his skin, he shifted her subtly so that she lay heavily over him, her legs spread on either side of his hips, just above where his arousal ached for more intimate contact.

The hitch in her breathing grew more pronounced as he drew her legs up. Reaching down, he found the sweet moist apex of her thighs, and her chest expanded deliciously against his when he explored her desire.

'*Salman…*' she shuddered out on a low, sleepy, husky moan, and that alone nearly drove him over the edge. He found her mouth and plundered the sweet depths, revelling in her sleepily sexy response.

With a subtle movement he replaced his fingers with his erection and, holding her hips fast, rocked up and into her, thrusting in and out with ruthless precision until her stunning eyes were open, looking into his. After long minutes of stringing out the torture for as long as she could last, Jamilah bit her lip and with her head thrown back splintered around him, sending him careening into an explosion so intense it took long minutes to float back down.

Sex. He could deal with this. Not the other. He just had to keep it all about sex.

CHAPTER TEN

Two evenings later Salman looked at Jamilah across the table, and she flashed him a teasing glance. He felt something intensely light bubble up in his chest, even as that ever-present desire pounded through him in waves.

He cursed himself for the clothes he'd brought for her. She was dressed tonight in a softly ruched silk dress, with thin spaghetti straps and a low neckline. It clung to her curves and fell in folds to her knees, revealing her shapely calves and slender bare feet. She was all the sexier for not wearing shoes. Her hair was piled untidily on top of her head and she wore not a scrap of make-up.

Only that afternoon, as they'd lain in a secret glade by a nearby pool, naked after a swim, she'd leant over him and taken him into her mouth, sending his mind into orbit even as he'd tried to stamp a control on his body that he'd never had to enforce before. But despite his ragged entreaties she hadn't stopped until he had lost all control and had been at her mercy completely. He'd never forget that self-satisfied sexy grin on her face. As if it was her mission to punish him for bringing her here in the first place.

Jamilah looked at Salman with wry impatience now,

bringing him back to the present with a jolt. 'Every time I talk about anything remotely personal you clam up.'

Salman sent her a warning look from across the lavishly decorated and heaving dinner table. 'I think I've already spoken far too much.'

'Yes,' Jamilah persisted with a gentle voice, 'about something that happened to you when you were a child... But what about everything else? Nadim? Your life so far?'

Salman found himself constricting inwardly. He knew he'd been avoiding talking about anything too personal—he already felt as if Jamilah knew far too much. His voice was brisk. 'There's nothing to tell. It's quite mundane and boring. I wanted to get out of Merkazad since I was eight years old, I've blamed Nadim on some level my whole life for what happened, which I know is irrational, and I've made a disgusting amount of money.'

He smiled then, and Jamilah shivered slightly.

'Don't try and psychoanalyse me. My life so far is exactly as you once said: *soulless*. And that's the way I like it.'

Jamilah knew she should stop and take the hint, but she couldn't. 'So, what? You won't be hurt again? That's impossible, Salman. We open ourselves to hurt every minute we're alive, but also to incredible joy.'

Salman was stuck for words for a moment. The concept of incredible joy was an alien one to him, and yet hadn't he caught a glimpse of it here with Jamilah? He shook his head mentally. Joy was not for him. He didn't deserve it. He was determined to wrest back some of his sorely lacking control. She was pushing him too close to an edge where his whole world threatened to drop away into an abyss.

Salman came out of his chair, and in a smooth move

Jamilah never saw coming plucked her effortlessly out of her chair, into his arms, and over to the bath behind the screen which had been prepared while they'd been eating.

Jamilah blushed to imagine what the villagers must think of them. Even though she knew she was putting on a good show of confident bravado to Salman, she was still quaking inside—sure he'd seen through her gauche attempts to make it appear as if she was in control of what was happening.

The past two days had slipped by with such deceptive ease that it scared her. They truly were cocooned in a tiny bubble of sensuality. The outside world could be going up in flames for all they knew or cared. And did Jamilah regret giving into Salman for one moment? As he undressed her now, with delicious intent, she felt some dim and distant regret, but told herself once again that she would think of it when this was over and she was back in Merkazad, in the real world, getting on with her life. She would have the rest of her life to regret.

Salman instructed her to get into the bath with a note of steel in his voice, and Jamilah responded with a delicious shiver of anticipation.

She watched as he too disrobed and stood there, powerful and intimidating. 'I want you to touch yourself like you did the other night,' he said.

Jamilah groaned softly. He was going to make her pay for what she had done to him earlier, in the glade. She'd noted the glint of determination in his eyes at the time, and now it was payback. She found the soap and let the magic of this moment out of time suck her under again, giving in to the heady pleasure and telling herself weakly that she'd let the questions go unanswered for now.

* * *

The following morning, early, Jamilah sat on a bench outside the tent and saw some of the local boys tending to the horses in nearby enclosures. She quirked a wry smile at the memory that she'd threatened to escape on one the other evening, when she'd arrived, and how Salman had autocratically declared that he'd forbidden anyone to let her take one.

Her smile faded, though, when she went inwards to the thoughts that had been plaguing her ever since Salman had fallen into a deep slumber beside her. She'd envied him his ease of sleep. It was day three. They were due to go back to Merkazad. And Jamilah knew she had two options open to her: she could avoid Salman again, for all the good it would do for her mental health, or she could try and take things further, but in the process risk much much more. She risked everything with that option—risked being hurt all over again.

She knew that if she insisted on pressing him to open up even more, he'd push her away for good. At least that was the gamble. Even as she accepted the futility of wanting that, a small, ever-persistent and ever-optimistic voice pointed out that things were different this time. This Salman was a different Salman from the one she'd known in Paris.

She sighed deeply. She couldn't stop the hopes and dreams. Was she on some level hoping for him to be cruel again? To reject her brutally? Wishing for a sort of punishment for having allowed herself to be so stupid as to believe that he might have changed? Her mouth tightened. She certainly deserved it, if that was the case.

She heard a movement come from inside the tent and resolutely stood up, mentally steeling herself for the exchange to come.

Salman had woken up to find Jamilah gone. He was

pulling on a pair of discarded jeans when she appeared in the doorway, dressed in her own jeans and a shirt. The village girl had returned them yesterday, washed and ironed. A frisson of unease went down his spine when he saw the familiar tilt to her chin and the crossed arms.

'Good morning.' His voice was still husky from sleep, and he could see how Jamilah's arms tightened fractionally, as if it had affected her. Immediately blood thickened and rushed to a strategic part of his anatomy. Pushing aside any niggles of inexplicable apprehension, Salman strode over to where Jamilah still stood, just inside the entrance, as if she were about to bolt.

He caught her face in his hands and pressed a kiss to her mouth, willing her to soften and relax into him. But she was rigid. He pressed a hand down her back to her bottom and pulled her into him, but to his chagrin she fought and pulled back, out of his arms.

'*No,* Salman. We're done with this. We're done here. Three days—that was it. We go home today, and I'm not going to go through this again with you. This time it is over. Really over.'

Salman looked at her and tried not to let those huge pools of blue affect him. He felt tight inside. 'Why does it have to end, Jamilah? I fail to see why when we're so good together. Why would you want to do that to yourself?'

'Because I'm trying my best not to be a complete masochist, Salman. You hurt me badly once before, and I'm not going down that route again.'

Salman felt sick inside. 'But it's not the same this time. We're different—*you're* different. You know why—'

'Why *what,* Salman? Why you rejected me in Paris

even though you didn't want to? Well, you did…and I have a confession now, too.' Her heart thumped ominously. 'I *was* in love with you. And it hurt me more than I can tell you. I'm not a robot, Salman. Perhaps it's easy for you to keep your feelings on ice and locked away, but I can't promise that…'

Salman felt anything but cold at that moment. He felt heat rising, because Jamilah had just told him she *had* loved him. He ran a hand through his hair impatiently, loath to keep on this track, afraid of what she might say…

Feeling desperate, as if something precious was slipping out of his grasp, and not liking it, he said, 'Stay here with me for another few days…until Nadim comes home. We don't have to deal with anything till then.'

Jamilah shook her head, her eyes huge and boring all the way to his soul. 'No. We have to deal with this now. All you're asking for is a stay of execution. I'm not interested in prolonging an affair that's just about sex. We have a relationship, whether you want to admit it or not, and relationships are about intimacy. Telling each other things, opening up. Nothing has really changed from six years ago, and when you walk away again, back to your life and your other women, I'll be right back to square one.'

Anger was like a tight knot deep inside Salman— anger at himself, for having indulged his weakness for Jamilah again. 'What do you want, Jamilah? More sordid tales of what happened to me? Like the fact that one day the soldiers brought out one of the maids from the castle and *used* her to give me a demonstration of what a man did with a woman? Is that what you want? Is that what will allow us to continue this affair?'

Salman saw how Jamilah paled, and immediately he

cursed and wanted to claw the words back. He'd had no right to tell her that. He'd already burdened her with too much. But even as he watched she composed herself and stood up tall, colour slashing her cheeks.

Jamilah shook her head sadly. His words *this affair* were lancing her inside. She was doing the right thing. That was all it was to him—all it ever would be. 'I'm sorry, Salman, truly sorry that you had to see that. But I'm not talking about that kind of intimacy. I'm talking about something that grows between two people in a relationship who…who care for one another, and you just won't admit that we have that. I'm talking about the banal details of our lives, our hopes and dreams.'

She had no idea how monumental what she asked was. Salman reached out to take Jamilah's shoulders in his hands, barely aware of what he was doing. 'You ask too much. It's an intimacy I'm not prepared to indulge in with anyone. I *can't.*'

Shock and renewed pain cut through Jamilah like a serrated knife-edge. She wrenched free of Salman, tears blurring her vision and slipping down her hot cheeks. 'I know the horrors you faced, Salman, and I can imagine how they made your belief in the fundamental goodness of man disappear. But it doesn't have to be like that again. What happened to you doesn't happen to everyone, and it's not to be expected.'

Salman's face was stark. He sneered, 'How can you possibly know what it's like?'

Jamilah put out a hand. 'Exactly—how *can* I know, unless you tell me?'

Unconsciously she put a hand to her belly.

'It's not that you can't indulge in that kind of intimacy, Salman, it's that you just *won't.* And all the sex in the world can't disguise that. I don't know why I let you believe that my baby wasn't yours, Salman, when you need a good dose of reality. *But it was!*'

She tried to dash tears away ineffectually, not even noticing the way Salman had paled. 'I know that must be hard to take—a man of your supreme control failing in one crucial aspect. But the fact is that it *was* your baby, and mine, and it died before it had a chance to live.'

The awful remembered pain nearly crippled her. She was livid with herself for being so stupid all over again. She was so angry she lashed out with words designed purely to wound and hurt as *she* hurt. 'Do you know what? I'm *glad* that baby didn't live, because you would have made a terrible father, Salman. You're an emotional wasteland, clinging onto your past like a shield, and you don't even deserve to be loved.'

Salman watched, stunned and in shock, as Jamilah fled outside. Her words had fallen like little arrow tips all over his skin. A baby. *His* baby. It wasn't possible. Medically, it wasn't possible. If it was any other woman he would automatically negate what she'd said, but it was Jamilah. She wasn't like that. She wouldn't lie. And, as if to compound the suspicion that she could be right, the doctor's words came back to him as if it were yesterday.

'You'll need to come for regular check-ups to make sure the operation has been successful. There shouldn't be a problem, but as with anything else there's a small failure rate.'

Recrimination burnt through him. Salman had naturally gone to the doctor with the highest success rate in his field. Once he'd had the operation he'd been supremely confident, and he'd been supremely busy. Of *course* he hadn't gone for any follow-up appointments… so it was very possible that the operation might indeed have failed. He had a sick feeling that if he went to get checked out that was exactly what he would find.

His head bursting and reeling with this knowledge, Salman remembered the hurt look in Jamilah's eyes the night she'd told him of the miscarriage. He'd thought it had been for the loss of the child, not because he hadn't recognised that it had been his. He cursed himself. Blindly, he went outside to follow her, but couldn't see her anywhere. He cursed again, and then heard a thunderous sound. Jamilah appeared from one of the enclosures on the back of a horse, hair streaming out behind her.

'Jamilah!' Salman shouted, furious with the fear that rose up even now to strangle him. He couldn't move, and could only watch as Jamilah cantered towards him, bringing the horse to a dramatic stop just feet away. Salman could feel clammy sweat break out on his brow. He'd never felt so weak in his life, and he detested that weakness.

A wealth of sadness rang in Jamilah's voice. 'At least I know you won't follow me, Salman. I'll come back when I hear the helicopter, and not before.' She whirled the horse around on the spot with an expert precision that even Salman could appreciate, and in a flurry of dust she was gone. Far away from him.

For hours Salman paced up and down outside the tent, his face as black as thunder. He'd issued orders and now waited for them to materialise. No one came near him, and there was no sign of Jamilah.

When the helicopter finally arrived he breathed a sigh of relief. Now she would come back, and he would talk to her. He knew now that he had to at least give her some kind of explanation.

The chopper pilot checked in with Salman. Time

went past with no sign of Jamilah. Salman felt rage building upwards, and wondered if she'd been stupid enough to try and ride all the way home. Then he reassured himself. She wouldn't have—not without provisions. Jamilah had local knowledge, and while their country might not consist of the more traditional desert, its rocky and mountainous topography held just as many dangers as an undulating sea of sands.

Just then Salman saw a young boy, leading a horse by the reins. It was the horse Jamilah had been on. With a different kind of fear constricting his insides into a knot, he strode over, learning that the boy had found it wandering in the village shortly before. Salman's insides curdled. It had come back without Jamilah.

Shouting orders—and an urgent one for someone to find the local doctor—and ruing the decision he'd made to bring Jamilah out here in the first place, Salman gritted his jaw against the onset of panic at what he was about to do. He swung himself onto the horse's back. He knew the chopper was nearby, but the horse itself would be the quickest way back to Jamilah's exact location. He would call the pilot and navigate him in if he needed to.

He hadn't been on a horse since the age of eight, but up until that time he'd been a more proficient horseman than even his own brother. Now he depended on knowledge he'd long since buried, nudging the horse in the direction it had taken with Jamilah and praying that it would take him back to her. If anything had happened to her— He blanked his mind. He couldn't go there.

The horse only started slowing down when it had cantered for about half an hour on the other side of the village. Miles from any habitation. This area was far from the lush oasis he'd left behind, and was as arid and rocky as the moon.

'*Jamilah!*' Salman's voice was hoarse from roaring her name.

He stopped the horse and turned it round and round, despair starting to snake into his veins even as he denied it. There was nothing remotely human as far as the eye could see. He knew the search party he'd commandeered wouldn't be far behind him, and they would have supplies, but there were treacherous rocks everywhere. A sudden mental image of Jamilah lying unconscious and bleeding made him squeeze the horse into a trot again as he called out her name for the umpteenth time.

And then he heard it—faint but distinct. '*Go away!*'

Salman's head went back. He closed his eyes for a moment, and the relief that went through him was nothing short of monumental.

He nudged the horse in the direction of her voice. 'Jamilah, *habiba,* where are you?'

'I'm *not* your *habiba.* Leave me alone. I'm fine.'

Salman followed the voice easily enough, and jumped off the horse when he saw a familiar, albeit dusty figure sitting on a rock, long tendrils of black hair loose over her shoulders. He made sure to tie the recalcitrant horse to a lone tree before walking over to her. She was looking resolutely away from him with arms crossed, and he sucked in a breath when he saw blood and a nasty bump on her forehead.

'You're bleeding.'

Salman's voice was like a balm to Jamilah's ravaged emotions, but at the same time she wanted to stand up and rant and rail and beat her fists on his chest until he might feel even a smidgen of the pain she felt. She sniffed, finally allowing that she'd been far more scared than she was letting on. 'The horse got spooked by an eagle and threw me. It was gone before I could get up.'

Salman was in front of her now, and to her chagrin all Jamilah could think about was how wrecked she must look. She still wouldn't look at him. His big hands were gentle, probing and touching her, smoothing back her hair to see the bump. She uncrossed her arms and slapped his hands away ineffectually, but she might as well have been swatting a fly. She heard the ripping of material and felt him press something damp to her sore head. She sucked in a breath.

Feeling very thirsty, but loath to admit it after doing something as immature and foolish as haring off on horse into the unknown with no supplies whatsoever, she gasped with relief when she felt an open water bottle being pressed to her mouth, a hand on the back of her head.

For the first time she let her eyes meet Salman's. She choked on the water; he looked wild. His eyes were very dark and his face was pale. He was covered in dust. He was encouraging her to take more water, and as she did so he said throatily, 'I'll save the lecture on running off so irresponsibly on a stupid horse for later. How sore is your head? Do you hurt anywhere else?'

Jamilah said meekly, 'I glanced my head off a rock. It's just a bump.' She saw how Salman's face paled even more. And then she said hurriedly, when that set off butterflies in her belly, 'I think my right ankle is sprained.'

He crouched down at her feet and peeled up her jean-leg. Her foot was indeed swollen above her sneaker and he gently took it off—and the sock. Jamilah winced with the pain as her ankle seemed to balloon before their very eyes.

Salman looked up at her and the set of his face was grim. 'We need to get you back to Merkazad.'

He lifted her up into his arms, and it was only then that Jamilah saw how he'd got there. She'd been too intent on ignoring him before.

'You came on the horse,' she said stupidly, her arm tightening fractionally around his neck.

She felt Salman's chest move. 'Don't remind me.'

With infinite gentleness and awesome strength he placed her in the saddle, and then with seemingly effort-less grace he smoothly vaulted on himself, behind her. The horse was skittish, and pranced, but Salman took the reins and brought him back under control swiftly. Jamilah was too stunned by this side of Salman she'd never seen before to say a word, but clearly he was an innately talented horseman.

The revelation almost, but not quite, distracted her from the sensation of Salman's rock-hard chest behind her, his powerful thighs cupping hers, and his arms en-casing her within their embrace. She felt safe, protected and cosseted, and yet again she was proving to herself that she'd learnt nothing.

They encountered the search party along with the local doctor not far from the village, and Salman di-rected the doctor and the girl who'd tended Jamilah that first night to follow them, thanking everyone else for coming to their aide, and telling them they could now relax. He sent one of the boys to tell the chopper pilot to get ready for take-off.

Jamilah's heart turned over as she heard how innately regal Salman sounded. He seemed to be morphing in front of her eyes into the man he was always born to be.

Within minutes Jamilah was being tended to by the shy girl and the local doctor, whom she would have trusted any day over the hospital in Merkazad. He pronounced to Salman that she should have X-rays just in case, but that he didn't think her injuries were more than a sprain and a bump.

With her jeans cut to above the knee on her injured leg, her ankle bandaged and a plaster on her head, Salman carried Jamilah out to the Jeep which was waiting. Despite everything that had happened, as they took off in the helicopter a short while later she felt an awful welling of emotion at leaving the little oasis, her eyes smarting with tears. She turned her face from Salman, terrified he might see her emotion.

Salman was grimmer than he'd ever been in his life. Jamilah had nearly killed herself in her attempt to get away from him, and he'd just found out that he'd been a father for the shortest amount of time—and the knowledge wasn't sending the sickening rejection to his gut that he might have expected. On the contrary, he felt a sense of *loss*. He glanced at the woman to his left. She was looking away from him, with her body angled away as far as possible.

He sighed. If there had been a moment in the past few weeks when Jamilah might not have hated him quite as intensely as she had since Paris, he'd well and truly quashed it.

'Salman, go away. You don't need to be here.'

He was implacable. 'Well, tough. I'm not going anywhere. And I *do* need to be here—you could have concussion.'

Jamilah sighed and wished her pulse would calm down. 'One of the girls can watch me.'

'*I'm* watching you. If it hadn't been for me you never would have gone off on that hare-brained horse.'

Jamilah sighed again, recognising Salman's immovability. He was sitting on a chair by her bed, arms on his knees, hands linked, watching her intently. She lay back and closed her eyes, hoping that if she feigned sleep he might leave. But knowing he wouldn't.

They'd gone straight to the hospital in Merkazad that afternoon, where Jamilah had been probed and X-rayed to within an inch of her life, all while Salman had issued autocratic orders and insisted on lifting Jamilah from place to place as if she were a complete invalid.

And now she was ensconced in the royal suite at the castle, having been bathed as well as she could be with her ankle bandaged, and fed a delicious dinner. All under Salman's watchful supervision. Only the shocked look from Lina, Iseult's personal maid, had stopped Salman from coming into the bathroom while she'd been washed.

For a long moment nothing was said, and tension escalated in Jamilah's body. When Salman spoke it was almost a relief—until she registered what he'd said.

'There's a good reason why I didn't think your baby was mine.'

Jamilah replied testily, 'Yes, because you arrogantly believe yourself to be infallible, and couldn't conceive for a second that something so human could happen to you.'

Jamilah heard him emit a short, curt laugh, but it came from the end of the bed where he now stood. Her eyes flicked open and her heart spasmed when she saw the pained look on his face.

'You're not far wrong in your analysis…but there was a bit more to it than that.'

Jamilah frowned, fingers unconsciously plucking at the ornately decorated coverlet on the bed. 'What do you mean?'

Salman ran a hand through his hair. 'The fact is that I made sure never to be susceptible to such a human failing. I made a decision a long time ago never to have children.' He sighed heavily. 'To that end I had a vasectomy when I was twenty-two. I spoke with the doctor who performed the operation today, while you were having your X-rays, and he informed me that there was every possibility it could have failed—and I wouldn't know as I've never been for follow-up checks.' He quirked a smile, but it was hard. 'Thanks to that arrogance you mentioned. I'll have to have tests to make sure, but after what you've told me, I think I know what they'll find…'

Shock coursed through Jamilah. No wonder he'd not believed it could have been his baby. This turned everything she'd thought she knew on its head, and threw up a whole slew of other implications that she didn't want to think about now.

She watched as he came back around the bed and sat down again heavily in the chair. An air of defeat clung to him, and he looked tired. A million miles from the cool arrogance he portrayed so well. 'Why did you do that?'

He looked down for a long moment before looking up, and the darkness in her eyes nearly made her want to say, Don't tell me if you don't want to. But she didn't. She was too weak—she wanted to know.

'Because,' he began, 'I never wanted any child of mine to go through what I'd gone through, and I believed that somehow the horrors I'd witnessed might be passed down, like some form of osmosis, in my DNA. I feared that I might not be able to protect my own child from evil, as my own father had failed to protect me.'

For a long moment neither one said anything, and then Jamilah said quietly, 'You must know now that that won't happen.'

The bleakness in his eyes reached out to envelop her. 'That's just it. I don't know. How can I know? How can anyone know? And I'm not prepared to risk such a thing. Not for anyone.'

Pain lanced Jamilah inside—so acute she almost called out. Because right now she harboured a secret. She held within her the living proof that Salman's seed lived and was healthy. She'd found out in the hospital earlier, when the nurse had done a routine pregnancy test as a precaution before the X-rays.

But how could she tell him? How could she be the one to stop him doing what he felt was right? After the horrors he'd seen, she couldn't blame him. With her heart breaking into pieces inside her, she asked fatefully, 'Even now you can't trust for a moment?'

He shook his head. 'I won't put anyone through living with me only to hope for more…' His voice was fierce. 'I won't do that to you, Jamilah. You deserve better than me. You deserve someone who can love you.'

Tears clogged her throat and burned behind her eyes. She turned her head away and choked out, 'Leave me alone, Salman. I don't want to see you any more.'

After a long moment of silence, she heard him get up and say heavily, 'Nadim and Iseult are coming home tomorrow.'

Jamilah was silent. She couldn't speak.

'I'll be leaving tomorrow evening…I have business to attend to.'

Emotion was rising within Jamilah, and she was afraid she'd crumble completely. '*Go,* Salman—just go.'

A deep sigh came, and then he said, 'I'm sorry, Jamilah. For everything. I'll have Lina come in to watch you…'

CHAPTER ELEVEN

SALMAN stood on Nadim's terrace and looked down over Merkazad. This view didn't threaten him any more. The emotions roused by the woman sleeping just a few suites away did.

He slammed a fist down on the stone balcony. He was a coward. He'd never felt more like a coward in his life. He wanted to go back into that room and seduce Jamilah until she was weak and pliant in his arms, until she admitted that she wanted him to stay, or until she said she'd go back to France with him.

But that was the one thing he couldn't and shouldn't do. He'd had countless moments to redeem what was left of his soul, and this was his last chance. He *had* to let Jamilah go, and never, ever pursue her again.

Even the thought of never seeing her again made him weak. But he stood tall and forced ice into his veins. Forced out all emotion. It was hard. It had been easy for so long to be unemotional, and now it was hard. He felt a flash of anger for the woman who had precipitated that painful thaw. But the anger dissolved just as quickly and was replaced by something much more poignant.

'Are you sure you're okay? Something about you is definitely different.'

Jamilah looked at her friend, and cursed the

Irishwoman's intuition. She felt herself grow hot under the narrowed amber gaze. Nadim and his wife Iseult had returned the previous day from their trip to Ireland. With their return, and the reality of a new royal baby arriving soon, the people who had been voicing discontent about Nadim's foreign wife seemed to have put aside their concerns.

Jamilah muttered something incoherent, and felt awful that she couldn't confide her secret. But at this stage—only scant days into her pregnancy—she was too superstitious after the last time. She felt vulnerable in the bed that she was still consigned to, wanting to escape Iseult's probing, and then it got worse.

She heard her say casually, 'Salman went home last night.'

'Yes?' Jamilah tried to sound as non-committal as possible. She'd feigned sleep when he'd come into her room late yesterday afternoon, but she'd felt the merest hint of a touch against her cheek, as if he'd trailed a finger down it, and it had taken all her resolve not to reach out and grab his hand and beg him not to go.

Iseult continued. 'He's been talking to Nadim about what happened to him as a child…I think they're finally going to be okay. And Salman seems to be interested in helping him run things here on a more regular basis.'

Jamilah's heart spasmed in her chest. If Salman was going to be a more regular visitor then surely that would have to be *good* news for his son or daughter? But the bittersweet prospect of it nearly made her want to double over with pain.

She forced a bright smile to her face. 'I'm really glad for them. It was time Salman shared what happened. It was too big a burden.'

Iseult's eyes narrowed even more. 'So you knew, then?'

Jamilah flushed, and cursed her big mouth. 'Yes... I... He told me.'

Iseult put out a hand. 'Jamilah—'

Jamilah took it and squeezed, barely able to cling onto control. 'Please, Iseult...not now. I'll talk to you about it again. I'm quite tired, actually...'

Iseult just looked at her and finally nodded, hauling herself up with an effort out of the chair. 'Okay. You know where I am.' She smiled ruefully, then said with a pointed look to her belly, 'I won't be going anywhere fast.'

Jamilah appreciated the attempt at humour, and gave her friend a quick tight smile. She watched as she left the room and then lay back, staring at the ceiling, wondering if she'd ever feel whole again.

A week later it was early evening, and Jamilah was back at the stables and hobbling around with a crutch to aid her. She didn't hear the Jeep come to a halt behind her, but she happened to look up and see Abdul's face in the far corner of the stableyard. His eyes had grown huge.

Jamilah frowned. 'Abdul...?' She turned to follow his gaze. When she did, she had to hang onto her crutch with two hands.

Salman was emerging from the Jeep, white-faced and with a grim expression. Just then a stablehand led a horse into the yard, just feet away from Salman, and she could see how he tensed and went even whiter.

But he stood firm, didn't move. Jamilah turned to face him fully, barely aware that Abdul had started to clear people and horses from the yard around them.

'Salman...'

He shut the door of the Jeep, and Jamilah only took in then that he was dressed in jeans and a loose shirt. He looked unkempt and tired, dark stubble lining his jaw. And her heart lurched.

He walked towards her, and Jamilah scrabbled back inelegantly, terrified that her composure would break. 'What…what do you want?'

Salman stopped a few feet away and quirked a brow. He looked weary, and a little sad. 'Somehow you never look pleased to see me, Jamilah.'

Her mouth twisted. 'Can you blame me?'

He shook his head. 'No, I guess I can't.'

'What are you doing here, Salman?'

'You could call it an intensive course in getting over my phobias—in getting over *myself*.'

Jamilah fought for equilibrium. She hitched up her chin. 'Well, good luck with that. But, if you'll excuse me, I have work to attend to.'

She turned and tried to walk away, but forgot for a moment that she couldn't walk. When she put weight on her sore ankle she yelped in pain and lurched helplessly into thin air, despite the crutch.

She was caught around the waist and hauled back against a hard, taut body. She felt Salman's arms tighten and his head came down, his mouth finding that spot between her shoulder and neck and pressing a kiss there. She moaned in despair at the inevitable rise of desire. And then with a struggle she fought to get free, twisting in his arms.

Salman eventually let her go, but she had to hang onto him, much to her chagrin, as the crutch had fallen. Her two hands were on his forearms, and she looked up at him, shaking her head. 'Why have you come back, Salman? What do you want?'

Sudden tears blurred her vision, emotion erupted, and she couldn't hold it back. 'Damn you, Salman, why can't you just leave me *be?* I don't want to be just your lover, or your mistress. I can't—'

Her words were stopped when he pulled her into him and his mouth covered hers in a searing brand. On a traitorous reflex Jamilah twined her hands around his neck and stretched up. This was both heaven and hell. She could taste the salty tang of her tears as they touched her lips.

Eventually Salman pulled back and looked down, smoothing a piece of hair from one hot cheek. 'Please… can we go somewhere to talk?'

Jamilah finally nodded. She couldn't deny this man anything when he stood so close and looked at her like that.

He lifted her up into his arms and asked gruffly, 'Where is your apartment?'

She directed him to the open door to her office, and then, once inside, through to the back, where her private sitting room and bedroom were. Carefully he sat her down on the couch, and then stood back.

Salman saw the wary look on Jamilah's tear-stained face, and felt pain lance his chest. And he welcomed it—even as he wanted to rip out his own heart for putting that wary look there. He took a breath. This would be hard, and he deserved for it to be as hard as possible— because he'd nearly thrown it all away.

'Will you just…hear me out?'

Jamilah muttered caustically, some of her fire returning, 'I don't have much choice. I'm a captive audience.'

Salman frowned. 'How is your ankle?'

'Fine…although I'm sure you didn't come all this way just to enquire after my ankle.'

'No.' Salman sighed heavily. 'No, I didn't.' He drove a hand through his hair, and then paced back and forth. Finally he stopped and looked at Jamilah. 'I didn't go home to France immediately. I went to Africa first—to the charity headquarters.' He grimaced. 'I thought I might distract myself there…but all it did was show me how lucky I am. What I could have if I only allowed myself to believe for a moment…to be brave enough.' He shook his head. 'Those kids…they have nothing. And no one. Very little chance to ever reclaim a normal existence.'

'Salman…?' Jamilah was confused.

He came and sat down—too close. But Jamilah had nowhere to go. He took her hand in both of his and she was shocked to feel a tremor.

'You broke something apart inside of me six years ago, Jamilah, and I wasn't ready to deal with it. But I've always known that some day I'd come back to you. It's as if I've always known you have that power. Ever since you were small…ever since that day at our parents' gravesides, when you were so silent and stoic…I felt then as if you could see right into me—and yet you weren't horrified by what you saw…'

A lump tightened Jamilah's throat again. 'I can't believe you remember that moment.'

He looked at her and her heart beat unevenly. 'I've never forgotten it. And the truth is, despite my stubbornness, even if I hadn't seen you again at the Sultan's party I would have found some way back to you…don't you see? I've been making my way back to you all along…'

Jamilah felt fresh tears welling. 'Don't, Salman—please don't say these things…if you're just saying this to persuade me back into your bed…'

He gripped her hand. 'I want so much more than that, Jamilah...I don't have any defences left where you're concerned. I flew to France from Africa, and a doctor confirmed that the vasectomy didn't work...he asked me if I wanted to do it again.'

Jamilah held her breath, her tears clearing. 'What did you say?'

He looked at her so intently she felt dizzy.

'I told him I'd have to think about it, and discuss it with someone.'

'Who?'

'*You.*'

Jamilah shook her head, and tried to stifle the flame of hope burning in her heart. 'But what do I have to do with it?'

Salman quirked a smile. 'Everything. Because there's no other woman on the planet I would contemplate having children with—only you.'

'What are you saying?' Jamilah wasn't even sure she'd got the words out, and somehow Salman was even closer, both her hands in his now.

'I'm saying that I've finally got it through my thick skull that I love you. I think I've always loved you. I can't live without you.' His smile faded then, and he looked more serious than she'd ever seen him. 'But with every-thing that's happened between us I won't be surprised if you don't want anything to do with me.' He took a breath. '*But*...if you could give me a second chance...I vow to spend my life making you happy, showing you how much I love you and need you... You're the only one who can possibly redeem my soul...'

Salman let her go and reached down to take some-thing out of his jeans pocket. It was a small velvet box, and he brought it up and opened it. Jamilah looked down to see a gloriously simple sapphire ring twinkling up at her.

'Jamilah, you would do me the greatest honour in the world if you would be my wife.'

For a second she couldn't breathe. She looked at Salman, and then reached out to touch his face with a shaking hand.

'This is a dream. You're not real.'

He grimaced slightly. 'I am real, and very flawed—as you well know… But you're the only one who has the power to make me even half-human again. Even though I know that I don't deserve this…*you*.'

Jamilah finally took a chance that this was real, and stepped into the unknown. She put aside the ring and took Salman's hand. She placed it over her still flat belly and said, with a quiver in her voice, 'You deserve it all. We both do. And it's already started… A new life is growing in my belly—a tiny part of me and you…proof that there is a future for us.'

Salman looked awed, shocked. His hand tightened on her belly. 'But…how? I mean…when?'

Jamilah shrugged and smiled tremulously. 'Who knows? When we were careless that time in Paris?'

For a moment Jamilah saw joy and wonder mixed with fear and trepidation in Salman's eyes, and brought his hand to her mouth to kiss it. Her heart ached, and she said with husky remorse, 'I didn't mean what I said that day at the oasis, about you being a terrible father, and my not wanting the baby. Losing the baby devastated me, and I always feared I wouldn't have another chance. I think you would be the best father in the world… I was angry and I took it out on you.'

Salman groaned softly. 'I deserved it—and so much more. But perhaps this really is our second chance.'

Jamilah sat up straight and took Salman's face in her hands. 'You've paid enough dues to last a lifetime, my love. You have just as much a right to happiness as the next man—*more*. You've done your best to heal your own wounds and have helped countless others to heal theirs. Don't you think it's your turn now?'

Salman looked tortured for a moment. 'But I hurt you so badly—the one person I should never have hurt.'

Fervently Jamilah declared, 'It was worth it, Salman. Every heartbreaking second was worth it if it's brought us here now.'

'Where is here?'

Jamilah could have cried at the doubt still lingering in his eyes. 'It's brought me to you, my darling. I love you, Salman. I always have and I always will. You and our baby. All I want is to spend the rest of my life being happy and in *love*. And, yes, I'll marry you…'

He kissed her long and deeply until she moved against him, seeking more intimate contact. Then he pulled back for a moment and declared softly, 'I vow to spend the rest of my life loving you and trying to be a good father to our child and, God willing, to any more children we may have…'

Jamilah put a tender hand on his jaw and said with quiet conviction, 'You *will* be a good father, Salman. Don't doubt it for a second.'

Neither one of them noticed when Iseult knocked softly and entered a few seconds later. They were too engrossed in each other. They also didn't notice when Nadim appeared, and grinned, before pulling his open-mouthed wife back from the door and shutting it softly behind them.

* * *

Two months later, in a flowing strapless ivory gown that cleverly disguised her growing bump, Jamilah was married to Salman in a small, private civil ceremony on one of the rooftop terraces of the Merkazad castle.

Nadim and Iseult stood witness, with their newborn son asleep in a carrycot beside them, sharing their own private looks of love. Salman and Jamilah had wanted to wait to marry until after the birth and christening of baby Kamil Sean.

And when the ceremony was over, just as the stars were beginning to come alive in the skies, Jamilah and Salman went off for a quiet moment by themselves, before they went down to greet the guests who were waiting to congratulate them in the castle's lavishly decorated ballroom for the formal celebration.

Salman stood behind Jamilah, his arms crossed firmly around her belly, her hands tangled with his. She sighed happily and leant back into his embrace as they looked out over the view of the magical Arabian city. In the far distance it was possible to make out the construction crane which marked the spot where they were building a huge children's fairground.

Salman had taken the brave decision to come forward as the public face of his charity, and share something of his own painful experiences—which he'd never thought he'd be able to do.

He kissed her head at that moment, and Jamilah smiled. They didn't need words. They were together, and that was all they needed—for ever.

CLASSIC

Quintessential, modern love stories
that are romance at its finest.

You can find more information on upcoming Harlequin® titles,
free excerpts and more at www.HarlequinInsideRomance.com.

HPCNM0112

REQUEST YOUR
FREE BOOKS!

Harlequin *Presents*

PASSION GUARANTEED SEDUCTION

2 FREE NOVELS PLUS
2 FREE GIFTS!

YES! Please send me 2 FREE Harlequin Presents® novels and my 2 FREE gifts (gifts are worth about $10). After receiving them, if I don't wish to receive any more books, I can return the shipping statement marked "cancel." If I don't cancel, I will receive 6 brand-new novels every month and be billed just $4.30 per book in the U.S. or $4.99 per book in Canada. That's a saving of at least 14% off the cover price! It's quite a bargain! Shipping and handling is just 50¢ per book in the U.S. and 75¢ per book in Canada.* I understand that accepting the 2 free books and gifts places me under no obligation to buy anything. I can always return a shipment and cancel at any time. Even if I never buy another book, the two free books and gifts are mine to keep forever.   106/306 HDN FERQ

Name _____ (PLEASE PRINT) _____

Address _____ Apt. # _____

City _____ State/Prov. _____ Zip/Postal Code _____

Signature (if under 18, a parent or guardian must sign) _____

Mail to the Reader Service:
IN U.S.A.: P.O. Box 1867, Buffalo, NY 14240-1867
IN CANADA: P.O. Box 609, Fort Erie, Ontario L2A 5X3

Not valid for current subscribers to Harlequin Presents books.

**Are you a current subscriber to Harlequin Presents books
and want to receive the larger-print edition?
Call 1-800-873-8635 or visit www.ReaderService.com.**

* Terms and prices subject to change without notice. Prices do not include applicable taxes. Sales tax applicable in N.Y. Canadian residents will be charged applicable taxes. Offer not valid in Quebec. This offer is limited to one order per household. All orders subject to credit approval. Credit or debit balances in a customer's account(s) may be offset by any other outstanding balance owed by or to the customer. Please allow 4 to 6 weeks for delivery. Offer available while quantities last.

Your Privacy—The Reader Service is committed to protecting your privacy. Our Privacy Policy is available online at www.ReaderService.com or upon request from the Reader Service.

We make a portion of our mailing list available to reputable third parties that offer products we believe may interest you. If you prefer that we not exchange your name with third parties, or if you wish to clarify or modify your communication preferences, please visit us at www.ReaderService.com/consumerschoice or write to us at Reader Service Preference Service, P.O. Box 9062, Buffalo, NY 14269. Include your complete name and address.

HP11B

Louisa Morgan loves being around children.
So when she has the opportunity to tutor bedridden Ellie,
she's determined to bring joy back into the motherless
girl's world. Can she also help Ellie's father open his
heart again? Read on for a sneak peek of

THE COWBOY FATHER

by Linda Ford,
available February 2012 from Love Inspired Historical.

Why had Louisa thought she could do this job? A bubble of self-pity whispered she was totally useless, but Louisa ignored it. She wasn't useless. She could help Ellie if the child allowed it.

Emmet walked her out, waiting until they were out of earshot to speak. "I sense you and Ellie are not getting along."

"Ellie has lost her freedom. On top of that, everything is new. Familiar things are gone. Her only defense is to exert what little independence she has left. I believe she will soon tire of it and find there are more enjoyable ways to pass the time."

He looked doubtful. Louisa feared he would tell her not to return. But after several seconds' consideration, he sighed heavily. "You're right about one thing. She's lost everything. She can hardly be blamed for feeling out of sorts."

"She hasn't lost everything, though." Her words were quiet, coming from a place full of certainty that Emmet was more than enough for this child. "She has you."

"She'll always have me. As long as I live." He clenched his fists. "And I fully intend to raise her in such a way that even if something happened to me, she would never feel like I was gone. I'd be in her thoughts and in her actions every day."

Peace filled Louisa. "Exactly what my father did."

Their gazes connected, forged a single thought about fathers and daughters…how each needed the other. How sweet the relationship was.

Louisa tipped her head away first. "I'll see you tomorrow."

Emmet nodded. "Until tomorrow then."

She climbed behind the wheel of their automobile and turned toward home. She admired Emmet's devotion to his child. It reminded her of the love her own father had lavished on Louisa and her sisters. Louisa smiled as fond memories of her father filled her thoughts. Ellie was a fortunate child to know such love.

Louisa understands what both father and daughter are going through. Will her compassion help them heal—and form a new family? Find out in
THE COWBOY FATHER
by Linda Ford, available February 14, 2012.

Love Inspired Books celebrates 15 years of inspirational romance in 2012! February puts the spotlight on Love Inspired Historical, with each book celebrating family and the special place it has in our hearts. Be sure to pick up all four Love Inspired Historical stories, available February 14, wherever books are sold.

SHLIHEXP0212

Harlequin®
Super Romance®

Discover a touching new trilogy from
USA TODAY bestselling author

Janice Kay Johnson

Between Love and Duty

As the eldest brother of three, Duncan MacLachlan
is used to being in control and maintaining an
emotional distance; as a police captain it's his job.
But when he meets Jane Brooks, Duncan soon finds
his control slipping away. Together, they fight for a
young boy's future, and soon Duncan finds himself
hoping to build a future with Jane.

Available February 2012

From Father to Son
(March 2012)

The Call of Bravery
(April 2012)

HSR71758

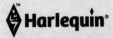
Harlequin®

n o c t u r n e™

NEW YORK TIMES AND *USA TODAY*
BESTSELLING AUTHOR

RACHEL LEE

captivates with another installment of

The Claiming

When Yvonne Dupuis gets a creepy sensation that
someone is watching her, waiting in the shadows,
she turns to Messenger Investigations and finds herself
under the protection of vampire Creed Preston.
His hunger for her is extreme, but with evil lurking
at every turn Creed must protect Yvonne from the
demonic forces that are trying to capture her
and claim her for his own.

CLAIMED BY A VAMPIRE

Available in February wherever books are sold.